THE DOUGHERTY REPORT

THE DOUGHERTY REPORT

FRANK TUMMINIA

MALEVOLENT BOOKS
Santa Monica, California

FIRST EDITION

Library of Congress Cataloging-in-Publication-Data is available on file.

ISBN: 978-1-936573-03-5

Malevolent Books, in association with Global ReLeaf, will plant two trees for each tree used in the manufacturing of this book. Global ReLeaf is an international campaign by American Forests, the nation's oldest nonprofit conservation organization and a world leader in planting trees for environmental restoration.

10 9 8 7 6 5 4 3 2 1

I would like to dedicate the book to my parents Paul and Phyllis Tumminia who taught me early on to never give up on my dreams.

THE DOUGHERTY REPORT

CHAPTER ONE

Lightning flashed across the moonless sky. Sheets of pounding rain bounced off the slick roadway like thousands of clear marbles. In the distance, the hum of an approaching car, the roar of it's racing engine, the skidding of its tires on the deserted road, was heard. From out of the darkness, a beat up Chevy came into view along with all the sights and sounds of a vehicle in distress. It sped down Mountain Cove fishtailing at every treacherous curve. Anna Payne's screams pierced the persistent splashing of the torrential downpour.

Her husband, Jonas, concentrated on the road and the challenges of the inclement weather. He had one hand fastened firmly on the steering wheel, the other stretched across the front seat caressing his pregnant wife's super extended belly. Jonas was in his early 30's, strikingly good looking with jet-black shoulder length hair. Anna's labor came on suddenly. Her light brown hair was sweaty and plastered against her puffy cheeks as she exhaled in increments prescribed by her Lamaze coach. Otherwise fair skin and porcelain complexion was now flushed and beading up with perspiration. She screamed again from her agony, squeezing her blue eyes shut and flapping around in her seat.

"Breathe baby," Jonas instructed. "Breathe."

Anna opened her mouth; there was a delay, a melodramatic pause, "something's wrong! I'm scared."

"Don't be! Hospital's just a couple of more miles."

Anna's expression said it all. She knew that they would not make it. She realized that she wouldn't see the inside of that emergency room. She accepted that it was punishment for crossing the line and that there would be no mercy for her on the other side.

"What will become of us, Jonas?"

Jonas looked up. His eyes quickly filled up with tears and his voice deepened as he mumbled something in Latin.

"Stop it!" Anna exclaimed breathlessly. "Don't blame him. It was our choice. We knew the consequences."

Anna's eyes bulged from the contraction. She screamed, a blood-curdling howl direct from the ninth circle of hell. "It's coming, Jonas. The baby is coming."

Desperately, Jonas turned the steering wheel sharply. The car veered off the road. Anna violently shifted in place. More screams. The Chevy stopped. Debris settled. Jonas reached over and attempted to push his wife's seat back. He struggled with the stubborn latch but it would not give. Jonas looked at the backseat. *Too God damn cramped*, he thought. Anna's shrieks intensified as did her impassioned pleas for relief.

The driver's door flew open. Jonas bolted out. He rushed around to Anna's side. Jonas stripped down to his hooded sweatshirt exposing the body of an athlete even through unflattering layers of clothing. Jonas draped his jacket down on the ground. Already drenched from the rain, he picked his semi-conscious wife up out of her seat and gingerly placed her on his leather bomber. Her legs immediately spread, hemorrhaging pink and purple innards that diluted with the soaking rain and ran on to the roadway in a slimy stream of discharge. Jonas dropped to his knees and placed his trembling hands between Anna's blood stained legs.

"PUSH!!!" Jonas ordered.

Anna obeyed with little objection. The top of the baby's head intrusively parted its mother's vagina, but not nearly enough.

"PUSH!!! Give it all you got!!!"

Anna pushed a final time. Her eyes flipped back and her petite body began to involuntarily shake. As Jonas retrieved the baby, lightning split the sky. A jolting burst of thunder announced the birth of their child. The sound of an infant crying filled the air.

Jonas cradled the newborn. He stared at the baby with wonder and awe.

"It's a girl," he declared in a prideful sigh. "You did it." Jonas showed Anna the baby. Through her tears of joy and pain, she managed to conjure up a smile, a final smile.

"We did it," she corrected her husband through clenched teeth. Suddenly, Anna's smile vanished. Pain returned with a vengeance. Her face contorted. Her body violently convulsed. Jonas gently placed the baby down. Anna looked up at her husband with disappointment. Her stare was vacant. Anna's crystal blue eyes transfixed before wandering up in their sockets. A glow emanating from her feet spread across her eerily still body, had extended to the newborn's umbilical cord. Her illumination was as radiant as she was beautiful. So intense was the light that Jonas had to shield his eyes. The baby's umbilical cord disintegrated. It's embers floated up and dissipated.

Crying, he scooped Anna up in his arms. Jonas looked up at the sky and muttered in Latin, "Don't do this! We hurt no one!!!"

A veil of darkness was sent fourth. Nothing was recognizable, except for Anna's incandescence.

"No. Don't leave me. Come back my angel. Come back!" Jonas begged to everyone, to no one. Anna's illumination ended abruptly as if someone had simply turned off the light switch. Jonas collapsed into her as she turned to sand in his embrace. Rain mixed with Anna's remains washed away into the muddy road.

Jonas stayed on his knees, crying hysterically. Both fists were full of his wife's granular remains. He watched, in disbelief, as the sand ran out from between his clenched fingers, like an emptying hourglass. Jonas slowly looked up and screamed at the heavens.

"Why? She was one of yours. Why?" His hollering echoed in the night. More lightning. More thunder. Jonas' eyes turned red and faded into the darkness.

With the baby's well being as inducement, Jonas got back into the car and drove away. The new father was frantic. There was a recklessness in his eyes. The baby slid wildly across the passenger seat. She was still wrapped in her father's jacket. Her crying had not subsided. Jonas pounded on the steering wheel.

"Does the baby need to be punished for our sins?" He asked again in fluent Latin. Jonas' rants continued as tears streamed down his face, "Where is the love of this God? Only a dark heart knows no forgiveness?" Suddenly, up ahead, the road forked and through the brush, an illuminated crucifix came into view. It was a House of God, in the middle of nothingness. Jonas hesitated, weighing his options, and then realized that there were no options. Jonas negotiated a hard right and the car took a two- wheel skid. Again the baby glided along the bumpy passenger seat.

The Chevy pulled up in front of the church. The church was dark. More lightning. More thunder. Jonas yanked his hood over his head and got out of the car. His palpitations began almost immediately, but Jonas disregarded his fears. His personal safety would have to take a back seat. He understood the implications of being in enemy territory, but like any good father, he ignored the dangers and focused on the business at hand. Jonas got out of the car and walked around to the passenger side. He gently removed the baby. Furious lightning. Fierce thunder. As Jonas walked toward the entrance, a savage wind kicked up. It's gusts knocked off his hood. Suddenly there were streaks of white throughout his jet-black hair. Jonas quickly covered up. With each step Jonas took his pain intensified. He winced. The closer he got to the mahogany door, his palpitations accelerated as he clutched the baby closer to his chest. He knocked. No reply. The pain from his brief contact with the door forced a single tear from his eye.

Jonas pounded on the door close fisted until he saw a light come on beyond the stain glass door pane. Jonas put down the baby. He hesitated and took one last look at the newborn. Sister Marguerite opened the door and peeked out, holding her bathrobe closed.

"Can I help you?" The sister asked barely above the howling wind.

For a fleeting moment, Jonas looked at the nun. His red eyes flared against his hidden face hugging the shadows.

"Take care of my little angel".

Jonas backed away and dissolved into the night. The rain stopped. The winds died down. Sister Marguerite looked down and immediately made the sign of the cross.

"Oh dear lord...," the nun gasped as she picked up the baby and brought her into the church.

The house of god was dimly lit, but it was warm and dry. Sister Marguerite set the baby down on a bench, in the closest pew. The infant immediately stopped crying. A long shadow consumed them both. It was Sister Eleanor, in her pajamas and polka-a-dot sleeping cap, rushing into the chapel and crossing an alter night-light.

"What is it Sister? Are you alright?" Eleanor asked wheezing as she barreled into the pew. "Be still my heart. But...?

"I have no idea," Marguerite shrugged.

"Should we phone the authorities?"

"Would you mind?" Sister Marguerite removed her bathrobe and began wrapping it around the baby. "I want to get the child out of these wet things. She'll catch her death."

Sister Eleanor spun around and ran toward the office as fast as her chubby legs could carry her. As Sister Marguerite undressed the infant, she made a discovery, a raised marking of sorts on the baby's tiny shoulder. Suddenly, there was a blinding flash of lightning. Accompanied by a blast of thunder so violent, it rattled the curtain rods on the confessionals. Confused, the nun ran her thumb over it. The bumpy impression remained in tact, uncompromising. Sister Marguerite put her reading glasses and leaned in closer to the child. The impression was that of a cross. Its tips were inverted arrow-like. The symbol's body: a clear circle with a half moon on both sides. The lower extremity of the marking was in the shape of an anchor.

Bleached out, through the colorblind mind's eye, the maternity ward at St. Vincent's hospital seemed hazy at best. It was filled with the precious sounds of babies crying. The sweet aroma of freshness, ever so pure. The nursery glowed with big, bold wallpaper decorations, bombastic balloons; clown faces and over sized lollypops everywhere. Rows of bassinets uniformly lined the window-encased room. Some newborns were sleeping soundly, others were fidgeting and still others were visibly annoyed that they were involuntarily yanked from their mother's 24-hour womb service. The agitated didn't mind expressing themselves by forcefully kicking their tiny legs against the very blankets they were cuddled under, in sporadic fits of protest. It was a magical place of bottles, baby power and Desitin. Beyond the innocence, an elevated nurse's station provided an over view of the infant's needs. A new delivery of formula sat on the granite top counter. Behind the neatly stacked boxes, Nurse Stella was on the phone to Carlo's Pizzeria ordering her belated dinner, when a stranger caught her attention. An uncomfortable sense of dread overwhelmed her; call it a maternal intrusion or the instincts of a health care professional with over 20 years on the job. But Nurse Stella immediately hung up the phone. Her Penne Vodka with a side of garlic bread would have to take a back seat. She had a potential situation.

"I'm sorry sir, visiting hours are over" she called out in an artificial drawl usually reserved for the hypothetical or dream like scenarios.

Arthur Shields ignored her and continued to stare at the babies devoid of the slightest expression. Shields was barely 20 years old with greasy, stringy hair that stuck to his sweaty freckled complexion. The stranger was dressed ominously. His faded jeans were benign enough, but it was his soiled army jacket, zipped up to his neck, during a sweltering august heat wave, that raised a red flag. Was it simply a wardrobe malfunction or something more sinister? Nurse Stella was not taking any chances.

"Sir, visiting hours are over. I'm afraid you're going to have to leave."

Shields disregarded the nurse. His pupils widened and remained transfixed as he continued to gawk at the newborns. He began to hum something vaguely recognizable, a chilling mix of a familiar lullaby and Green Day's "Good Riddance". Beads of perspiration invaded Arthur's forehead, like the yanks invaded the beach head at Normandy. The sweat irregularly slid down the side of his razor-stubbed face. He was getting closer to something, something unspeakable. An act of terror in the name of the father, the son and the Holy Ghost.

Frustrated, Nurse Stella stepped out from behind her station and walked toward a visibly nervous Arthur.

"Sir, I'm going to have to call security, if…"

"What's your name?" Arthur asked in a deep, maybe too deep for his age, shaky voice.

"Excuse me?"

"Tell me your name. Come on. What harm could it do?"

"Do you want me to get security?"

"Are you menstruating?" He asked with a half smirk.

"I'm calling security," Stella gasped, taken back by the strangers' crudeness.

"It's just I sensed an attitude," Arthur explained, "…and I was wondering if it's that time of the month for attitudes or if you are simply a bitch?"

The stranger quickly, and with a single swift downward motion unzips his army jacket, revealing sticks of dynamite evenly deployed around his bomb belt. Nurse Stella screamed, startling the infants as a chorus of crying broke out. Arthur removed a detonator and folded his long dirty finger around it. He brought the detonator to his lips. The stranger leaned into his clasped prayer-like hands and kissed the weapon of mass destruction….

Liam Dougherty gasped as he sprung up in bed. Dougherty was in his early 40's with dark brown hair that at the moment, suffered from severe bed head. He rubbed the nightmare from his tired blood shot eyes. Dougherty scratched his pesty perpetual five o'clock shadow with the same hand he scratched his nuts, not a half a moment ago. The facial hair, although in it's infancy stage, helped eclipse the lower half of a worn and beaten expression. His studio apartment was a shit hole by anyone's standards. Clutter hid the tumbleweeds of dust, grime and soot, but not necessarily in that order. It was the smallest apartment in the six family walk up located in the armpit of Newark.

Dougherty reached for his cigarettes. The night table was littered with sunflower seeds, money, and a half empty or half full depending on your level on pessimism, bottle of Jack Daniels. He found a spent pack of Marlboro lights. Desperately, he fingered through the overflowing ashtray searching for a butt, or joint, anything with a few drags left in it. Dougherty retrieved a crushed cigarette and lit it immediately. Suddenly the sound of a toilet flushing interrupted the outside sounds of the thriving metropolis below. The bathroom door opened. The smell of cheap perfume permeated the air. Stale tobacco and Listerine were also preludes to her grand entrance. Beatrix, aka *Ms. Hot and Spicy* according to the escort flyer walked out straightening her tight dress. Deceptive advertising, Madison Avenue at its best. Her flyer should have read: *Ms. Lukewarm and fidgety*, although she did personify the three B's: blonde, blue eyes and busty—very busty—enormously busty.

"Shouldn't smoke in bed," Beatrix warned rushing over to a mirror.

"Who are you, fire Marshall Bob?"

"Spent five years as a volunteer for the Absecon FD, just outside of Atlantic City."

"Is there no end to your talents?" Dougherty asked in a yawn.

Beatrix stared in the mirror, scrunching her wet hair. "Got a cautionary tale. Want to hear?"

"Do I have a choice?"

"One night we get a call from the Taj Mahal. This high roller was smoking in bed and fell asleep with an ash tray in his lap...remind you of anyone?" Beatrix motions in the mirror at Dougherty as she applies a generous amount of cherry red lipstick. "Wink. Wink. Anyhow, he burnt his pecker off." She took a dramatic pause, before continuing. "Hand to God, his little Soupy Sales melted right into the satin sheets."

Dougherty rolled his eyes. "Charming."

Beatrix puckers up, gives herself a final once over and struts over to the night table. "The moral of the story, you ask...?

"I didn't."

"Mind your Johnson and your Johnson will mind you." Beatrix scooped her money off the night table. "Damn generous of you lover, but nothing happened. That entitles you to a reduction. My "too poop to pop" rate." She throws some money back at Dougherty.

"Decent of ya." Dougherty said as condescending as condescendding gets. "But how will you get by?"

"Volume," the hooker winked. "Later lover," Beatrix blew him a kiss and walked to the door. She suddenly stopped and turned back to him confused. "Oh, who's Arty? You called his name a couple of times in your sleep."

"My mom." Dougherty replied without flinching. "Think that's odd? My father's name is Shirley.

"Whatever." Beatrix nodded in disbelief and walked out of the apartment.

Dougherty immediately extinguished his cigarette and once again attempted to rub the hangover from his eyes. His hand fumbled around Beatrix's side of the bed and fished out the remote from under the sheets. Dougherty sunk back down into the bed and turned on the television. Snow splashed across the nineteen inch Sony. He changed the channel, more snow. He made a mental note to place the cable bill closer to the top of the creditor's list. There was a knock on the door. Dougherty ignored it, hoping whoever it was would go away. For his sins, they did not. In fact, they knocked again, harder and longer. Dougherty turned off the television. He leaped out of bed in his shorts and cautiously approached the door.

"Who is it?"

"We're looking for Liam Dougherty…" A voice answered.

"We?"

"Monsignor Hayden sent us." Another voice chimed in.

Dougherty looked through the peephole and opened the door. Surprised, Fathers Leonard and Cobb, dressed in full priest garb, gave Dougherty the once over. Obviously, Liam was not what they were expecting.

"Liam Dougherty?" Father Cobb asked fearful of the answer. Dougherty nodded and opened the door wider.

"Father Liam Dougherty? Father Leonard confirmed.

"What do I have to do, recite the seven holy sacraments?" Dougherty sighs, before his tirade, "…let's see there's Happy, Sneezy, Sleepy, Grumpy, Bashful, and you gentleman. Come in, please."

The priest walked in apprehensively. They looked around the apartment at the maxed out ashtrays, the bottles of JD and of course, the piles of filthy dishes and pizza boxes in the sink.

"Excuse the mess, maid's day off." Dougherty walked back to the bed. "What can I do for you guys?"

"Monsignor Hayden wishes to see you immediately," Father Cobb explained.

"Well, I wish he would have phoned—"

"The Monsignor tried…," Father Cobb maintained. "Your service has been disconnected."

"Gotta have a word with my book keeper," Dougherty said incredulously. "Look, I don't know what you heard, but I'm done with this…"

"I'm afraid the Monsignor was very insistent," Father Cobb said.

"Monsignor Hayden suggested that if all else fails, to remind you that you owe him," Father Leonard added.

Dougherty shrugged. "He gave me a twenty dollar exacta at Aqueduct in 2002 and so now we're married?"

"I'm just the messenger," Father Leonard said humbly.

"So was Judas," Dougherty retorted.

"Please Father Dougherty. It's urgent," Father Cobb reiterated.

"But all the way to Trenton now?" Dougherty sighed. Just the thought of the car ride exhausted him. "Do you have any idea what traffic is going to be like?

Under a capricious sky, the Trenton Archdiocese stood well pronounced against the state capital's skyline. Much like the bell tower in Notre Dame, it provided a sanctuary for those who believed, the hunched back faithful that were brave enough to ring the bells in time of need. The dreary gray building sat across from the federal courts in the legislative section of town. The streets and sidewalks were filled with all the mid day hustle and bustle of a desensitized bureaucratic machine.

Beyond the Diocese's protective wrought iron gate, deep within the marble halls of excess, Monsignor Hayden's office was unobtrusively tucked away on the east wing of the second floor.

The office was plush with rich mahogany everywhere. Impressive floor to ceiling bookcases with volumes of bibles and other catholic redundancies, took up three of the four walls. It was nothing more eloquent than traditional Christian over kill. Monsignor Hayden was behind his massive circular desk. Hayden was in his mid 60's, authoritative looking even with his bad comb over. His eyes were soothing, having born witness to a lot of crazy shit. Some of which he believed. The rest? Well, the Monsignor maintained a patient *wait and see* approach. In Hayden's background, paintings of Pope John Paul the 2nd and Pope Benedict the 16th adorned the wall.

The wooden hand carved double doors opened with a winded creek from a rusty hinge, the noise eventually tailed off. Father Leonard and Father Cobb escorted Dougherty in. Liam was dressed casually but neatly in jeans, tee shirt and sport jacket. He looked more like a best selling author than a man of god. It was a far cry from his formal parish issued white-collar priest attire. As they walked toward the Monsignor, their chorus of footsteps echoed loudly on the shiny hardwood floor.

"Good of you to come Father Dougherty," Hayden offered with a welcoming smile.

"I was telling these guys, I've got to be back by 2pm, the Yankees are playing Boston."

Monsignor Hayden motioned to Fathers Cobb and Leonard. The priests walked out. Hayden extended an open hand invitation for Dougherty to sit across from him. Liam took the Monsignor up on it and was quite struck by the chair's vegetable tanned leather.

"So how have you been Liam?"

"Oh, you know," Dougherty stammered, "…nothing a little Zoloft and Valium couldn't fix."

"And the nightmares? Are you still having them?"

"They've taken a different form. I see naked clergy. Dreamt of you last week Charles. What a revelation. Talk about your burning bush."

Monsignor Hayden smiled calmly. "It won't work. You're not shocking me into signing your letter of resignation. I still believe you have a life in the church. Your work, your accomplishments under God are unprecedented. I employ you, do not deprive the church of your gifts."

"He was 20 years old, Monsignor, and under my care. It was my responsibility to recognize the signs."

"No one blames you for Arthur Shields' actions except you."

Dougherty grew increasingly more uncomfortable. He began fidgeting. "Let's cut to the chase, shall we? CC Sabathia is pitching this afternoon."

"The Archbishop, through his grace and the lord's intervention, has seen fit to entrust me with an intricate and somewhat covert function of this diocese..."

"The corner office, huh?" Dougherty interrupted, looking around. "I noticed. Does it come with a 401K plan?"

The Monsignor took a breath. He found Dougherty particularly exhausting that day. But with an unflinching eye on the big picture, Hayden continued, "I am charged with either validating or refuting metaphysical events. Document all spiritual incidents, mephistophelean episodes while weeding out secular occurrences."

"Fact or fiction, huh Charles?" Dougherty asked with his infamous sarcasm. "I can set the record straight right now, unequivocally fiction."

"Redefining good and evil now more than ever is an essential part of the lord's work, I assure you."

Dougherty checked his watch. "I hate to be a nudge, but what does this have to do with me?"

"There's room in the corner office."

Dougherty paused. "Are you offering me a job, Charles?"

"I'm offering you a chance to be a priest again. To be part of a grand purpose. Heed your lord's calling Father Dougherty. Let him in."

"Can I go now?" Dougherty sighed.

The monsignor settled back into his chair and took a long moment. A brief pause that gave Hayden ample time to climb off his soapbox, before it caved in and allowed for him to regroup. Like that annoying mosquito trapped in your bedroom and whistling in your ear on a sweltering summer night, Dougherty was beginning to bug him.

"An occurrence has recently been brought to my attention. I'd like you to take a look, evaluate and report directly to me. For your cooperation, I will not only approve your letter of resignation, I will personally contact Dean Wilson at Montclair State and recommend you to head up their Department of Theosophy…"

Dougherty looked at the Monsignor with surprise. The Monsignor continued, "…Yeah. That's right. I know about the professorship. I think you're short changing yourself, but it's your call."

"Again Monsignor, why do you want me?" Dougherty asked sincerely. "I'm not much of a Christian. Not much of anything."

"Besides your degree in psychiatry and vast clinical experience as a Theosophist?"

Dougherty shrugged. "Surely there are shrinks far more
passionate—?"

"Liam, you possess real world objectivity." Hayden
explained. "It is your detachment that is deficient in our rank
and file. We lack the ability to look outside the box and *that* is
our shortcoming."

Monsignor Hayden brought Dougherty into a dimly lit
observation room. They stood behind a two-way mirror. On
the other side of the mirror, was what appeared to be a little
girl's bedroom with a few glaring exceptions. There were high-
intensity blue electric rays burning down on a twin bed, creating
an iridescent haze that enveloped the bedroom. The lights were
suspended from heavy stainless steel brackets at all four corners.
The walls were mirrored in order to redirect the reflections and
maximize illumination. There was a constant hum from the
fans that kept MYRA cool in the glow of her cocoon. Myra
couldn't have been more than nine years old. She had perfect
features and tight ringlets of blonde shoulder length hair. But
even from that distance, Dougherty could see that the child was
frail looking as she sat at the foot of her blanket-less bed,
staring expressionless away from the onlookers, in panties and a

loose fitting pajama top. Myra's skin had an unnatural gold tinge to it. Dougherty immediately recognized her condition to be Crigler-Najjar Syndrome. It was extremely rare with only about 100 known cases worldwide. Crigler-Najjar was a genetic disorder that caused high levels of a toxin called bilirubin to build up in the body, resulting in severe jaundice that, if untreated, caused brain damage and eventually after a slow deterioration, death. An enzyme in the liver normally breaks down bilirubin. If the enzyme is missing, the toxin can be kept in check only by the wavelengths of blue lights. Hence, the elaborate set up.

"Crigler-Najjar Syndrome," Dougherty reaffirmed. "Her only hope of long term survival is a liver transplant."

"She's been on the list a little over a year now."

"How old is she?" Dougherty asked.

"Myra's nine. She came to us from St. Peter's orphanage."

The child slowly turned toward the two-way mirror. The whites of her eyes were yellow. Her stare, vacuous and sad.

"She hears us."

"Impossible," the Monsignor said.

"She knows we're here. Trust me." Dougherty opened her file and examined it, cherry picking his questions. "Home schooled. Normal academic development. How long has she been mute?"

"To the best of my knowledge, Myra has never uttered a word. Is it because of her condition?"

Dougherty put on his glasses and took a more in-depth look. "It's not characteristic of the disorder. MRI and CAT scans are normal—."

"Then why the silence?

"Didn't your mother teach you, if you don't have anything nice to say, don't say anything? Dougherty remarked.

"Myra never knew her mother."

"Then maybe she just doesn't like you. Where's the neurologist's report?"

As Dougherty buried himself deeper into the file, Sister Camille entered the child's bedroom. The nun appeared down right scary, ghoulishly phosphorescent in the blue hue. The Sister greeted Myra and walked her over to the two-way mirror.

"I don't see anything from neurology," Dougherty thumbed through the file. "Oh, here…Charles, get ready to make that call to Montclair State. A very sick introvert hardly qualifies as a stigmata."

The Monsignor nodded to Sister Camille. The nun opened the back of Myra's pajama top.

"No. But this might…" Hayden said motioning.

Dougherty looked up from the file. He slowly removed his glasses. Myra exposed a tattoo artist's masterpiece. An illustration of sorts that snaked across the child's entire back. The busy marking was involuntarily imprinting, in descending order right before Dougherty's eyes. It was as if someone was methodically writing on Myra's back from the inside out. Liam leaned in closer to the mirror and feasted on the visual splendor. Dougherty felt compelled to feed the beast, his own pathological curiosity. Liam may very well have been a drunk and drug abuser, but he was also a doctor. And what he was witnessing first hand was certainly one for the medical books. Clusters of symbols and groupings of hieroglyphics that were interwoven with Aramaic calligraphy. The marking's diversification was mesmerizing, astounding in fact. The actuality that it was involuntarily presented in living color.., fresh, stylized by a vividness that faded, and then flared with every breath the child took, it was simply mind blowing even to the most devout skeptic. Dougherty and Myra made eye contact. They locked stares. Their connection was instantly profound. He looked into her eyes, two discolored portals that gave him a glimpse into her tormented soul as Myra saw into his suffering as well.

CHAPTER TWO

Into the wee hours of morning, Dougherty stayed in his apartment slumped over his cluttered desk with his tired bloodshot eyes glued to the computer screen, dropping his stare only to input data. An exhausted desk lamp illuminated the dozens of photographs of Myra's tattoo in various stages of development. The uploaded images on his hard drive were being painstakingly dissimulated, scrupulously dissected and meticulously cross-referenced not only with religious encyclopedias, but also with bibles of the occult.

Dougherty concentrated only on a section of the impression in particular. The raised marking on her shoulder populated his 17-inch flat screen. It was a cross or sorts. Its tips were inverted arrows. The symbol's body was a clear circle with a half moon on both sides. The lower extremity was in the shape of an anchor. Dougherty superimposed a Christian cross. But it did not match. He reversed it, superimposing a satanic symbol and Dougherty got a positive ID. The symbols detached and were separately identified as a *"Camargue"* and the *"Triple Goddess"*. Their definitions splashed beneath each symbols respectively. Dougherty immediately printed the information as more of Myra's markings filled the computer screen. Dougherty withdrew a book of maps from the center of a shaky stack of books. He opened to the back of the publication, sliding his finger across the page and stopping at longitude and latitude.

"Look at you." A male voice filled the room. "You're passionate about something again. Congrats."

Startled, Dougherty looked up. Arthur Shields was sitting on his desk. Liam ignored him and got back to the business at hand.

"What's all this stuff?" Arthur persisted. "I'm talking to you Father."

"I'm not afraid Arty. You can't exist."

"Oh? Not only am I here, I'll let you in on a secret, one murderer to another, I'm here to stay."

"Go away!!!" Dougherty said forcefully.

"I kinda like being ringside to watch you screw up that kid."

Dougherty paused. He closed his eyes as a fit of trembling overtook him. Liam opened the desk drawer and removed a pill bottle. He quickly downed a handful of pills with a stiff belt of whiskey.

Arthur laughed. "Run to your pills. Turn to your whores. Hide in your bottles. It won't do you any good. Because I'm everywhere. I'm nowhere." Arthur slapped the pills and the whiskey off the desk. "Now what?" Arthur asked. "Prayer? Not an option. You denounced God, remember? Shame, cause faith does move mountains, Father. But you're a faithless sack. What do you have here?"

Arthur swaggered around the desk and stood behind Dougherty, looking over his shoulder at the computer screen. Arthur was quite taken by Myra's distinctive marking. "Well, lucky for you I took Aramaic in my senior year." Through the reflection in the monitor, Shields noticed that Dougherty's eyes are getting heavy. "Hey, Liam, no dozing. It's rude. I want you wide awake for this…"

Arthur extended his arm toward the exterior wall, and flipped his hand palm up until the wall crumbled with a mighty roar into the alley below.

Dougherty shook his head in disbelief. "That's coming out of my security deposit, I'm sure." Liam followed Arthur over to the great cavity where his wall stood only moments ago. Shields invited Dougherty to step out into the starry night. Apprehensive, Liam stood on the edge and looked down at the Newark shooting gallery. The vacant lot below was a druggie's paradise, lit only by the flickering glow of a garbage can's burning contents, where junkies hugged the shadows. Wandering crack heads, nomads pushing lopsided shopping carts filled with nothing and everything, and gang bangers decorated in their crew's color of affiliation, all looked up united while brushing off fallen debris.

"Well, what are you waiting for?" Arthur asked, his patience wearing thin.

Yeah, Liam what are you waiting for? Dougherty wondered as he struggled to put one foot in front of the other. He wasn't fearful of the 100-foot plunge, interestingly enough. Chances were good that a crack head would break his fall in the event things went terribly wrong. So it wasn't a mental issue. Dougherty wanted to take that step, he needed to take it, but he remained paralyzed. The old adage, "*the journey of a thousand miles begins with the first step*" raced through his mind. He could rationalize it until the cows came home, his body simply would not cooperate. Both his legs remained ridiculously heavy. But after a little nudge from Arthur, more like a shove, Dougherty was well on his way. Make no mistake; the adventure was far from a Peter Pan like flight to safety. In this never-never land, there were screams, panic, and chaos as Dougherty found himself on United Airlines flight 93 out of Newark airport, bound for infamy. The plane bounced wildly. Arthur and Dougherty were sitting in the last row. Arthur was having a grand time. He was basking in the ensuing tragedy; laughing and sipping Grey Goose, on the verge of busting out into a chorus of television show tunes and encouraging a sing-a-long. Dougherty was visibly frightened. His hands clung tighter to the armrests with every dramatic tip and shift the plane took. So much so the tips of his fingernails were white capped from the pressure. Three men of Middle Eastern descent, sporting red bandanas and wielding knives, marched up the center aisle terrorizing. The plane took a drastic nosedive. Suddenly everything not hunkered down became air borne and rocketed toward the cockpit. Carry-on luggage bounced around the cabin like basketballs in play. Passengers were thrown around. More shouting. More pleading. More praying.

"You don't look so good, father," Arthur remarked. "I prefer sitting close to the little boy's room. I have irritable bowel syndrome. Probably the only thing I haven't confessed to you."

An elderly woman attempted to get out of her seat. A terrorist slapped her back down. He yanked her hair and put a knife to her throat, while yelling something in Arabic. Arthur watched, and then called out to the madman. "Hey you," the terrorist looked at Arthur. "…How do you stop a suicide bomber from drowning?" Arthur paused. "Take your foot off his head."

Arthur began laughing as the terrorist approached him.

"Liam, click your heels and repeat after me, Afghanistan banana stand…"

The dynamic duo was instantly transported to a sidewalk café in the Indonesian island of Sumatra. The small restaurant was a popular tourist spot because of its proximity to the water. The quaint cobblestone street rear-ended against a flawless white sandy beach of epic proportions. Music played. Vacationers and locals partied to the pulsating beat of an Asian form of Salsa. Dougherty and Arthur ordered lunch against the backdrop of festivities. It was a welcome reprieve from the carnage at 30,000 feet, however short lived. As the earth belched under their feet, a silent but deadly hiccup came from the direction of the beach. The graduating roars of water flowed as if someone had turned on all the fire hydrants in the world at precisely the same time.

The escalating sound of fluid quickly intensified all out of proportion. It was obvious that screams would follow. Behind Dougherty's back, the North Pacific Ocean began to rise. A sleeping giant was awakened and swelled into a massive, solid wall of water. The rippling waves gained momentum like a thoroughbred racehorse thundering down the home stretch, as the Tsunami drowned everything caught in its destructive path.

Dougherty leaped out of his chair. "Let's get out of here!!!"

"Since I'm already dead," Arthur said, buttering his bread, "...I'm going to stay and finish my drink. But you knock yourself out."

Dougherty ran. He lost his footing at first, spilling onto the crowded street, careening and rebounding off the vast majority running for their lives. He sprinted up the boulevard as fast as his legs would carry him. Dougherty's breathing became labored, palpitations nearly tore a hole through his chest; his temples pulsating. It was no use. The 80-foot tidal wave was a heartbeat away. Dougherty felt wetness under his feet as he splashed through the spreading puddles from the wave's outer bands of water. Death was over his shoulder and sprinkling cool drops on his neck as it was bearing down on him. Dougherty did not look back. He didn't dare. Liam simply held his breath anticipating being swept away in a rush. The gamut had come full circle and there was silence. Abrupt, absolute silence and it was golden. Proving, once again, unequivocally Columbus' theory that the world was round.

Dougherty was somehow spared, plucked off the streets of Sumatra by divine intervention and placed in a deep freeze on a barren and frozen wasteland of nothingness as far as the frigid eye could see. Liam stood shivering in place and battling a bitter wind that pinched his exposed flesh like millions of tiny needles.

"I'm cold," Dougherty said barely above the whistling wind. He studied his frosty hand as it began to turn an unflattering shade of blue. "Can anyone hear me? I said I'm freezing."

Arthur's voice reverberated from everywhere. "Of course you are. This is the ninth circle of hell. You were expecting a Tahitian forecast?"

"Why am I here?"

"Because you, my friend, are an ingrate."

"Ingrate?" Dougherty repeated.

"You had a relationship with God. We were all envious. He allowed you to be his instrument. You turned your nose up at him. Now, a second chance later, you're still ungrateful."

Again, Dougherty looked at his hand. The blue was spreading, traveling across his forehead with the speed of light. "Why am I turning blue?"

"Being this far from the almighty will do that to a person. Just think of us as the original Blue Man Group." Arthur laughed. "You'll get used to the 'blue' jokes quickly enough. Anyhow, it's not all gloom and doom. There are perks."

"Perks?"

"Yeah. And you don't even need to ask. The dark one reads your lustful heart. The girls are on their way," Arthur assured him.

On the lost horizon, a legion of misshapen prostitutes appeared. The scantily clothed, damaged and discounted were blue as well and riddled with leprosy. Some strutted their stuff toward Dougherty. Others simply slithered, but the undesirables were not traveling in real time. So before Dougherty high tailed it out of there, the streetwalkers surrounded him.

"Unfortunately, down here, our passions become an abomination," Arthur laughed louder.

The prostitutes unfurled their serpent-like tongues in perfect synchronicity. Dougherty's screams faded into the frigid abyss.

Dougherty's head violently sprung up from his crowed desk with a pencil stuck to his sweaty cheek as the morning sun exploded into his apartment. Still startled by yet another night-mare, his entire body snapped back into the chair. The pencil fell off, leaving the word *Dixion* and the numeral *2* partially imprinted on his rosy cheek. He waited for some form of composure to find him. He was too dazed to go searching for tranquility at that hour of the morning. And when his eyes finally did focus on the clock, he realized it wasn't all that early and that he had fallen asleep while researching Myra's markings. And in the light of day, he understood that there was no such thing as the bogeyman and that there were no blue prostitutes with oily discharge. At least not in New Jersey. Dougherty instinctively reached for his pills. He hesitated, and then placed the pill bottle down. Liam had too much to do and staying grounded was probably a good idea under the circumstances.

The best idea he had in a long time. Dougherty found his cell phone under a shit load of photographs and dialed.

"Monsignor Hayden, please...," Dougherty said into the phone, with a morning voice.

Back at the Monsignor's office, Dougherty and Hayden were huddled around the desk, staring down at a photograph of Myra's marking.

"See this," Liam pointed. "It's a cessation. A dramatic pause, if you will. There's another down here. So we must take them as three separate scenarios..." Dougherty pulled out another photo. He uncapped his black sharpie and marked up the picture with bold, distinctive strokes as he went along. "The first scenario, of this photo, was taken of Myra's marking in mid August 2001. This cluster was a delineation of ancient mythologies emblematic of death and destruction. The upside down triangles represent right over might and the carnage would spew from the bowels of middle earth or of Middle Eastern descent. The stick figures symbolize the "docile" or the innocent and unsuspecting..."

"And these numbers here?" The monsignor pointed.

"At first, I thought they were Roman numerals. But it is instead, an algebraic equation. The answer is, the year of our lord, the product derived from a multiple of three..."

"Why three?"

"The blessed trinity," Dougherty explained. "The father, the son, and the holy ghost. It's the entire grouping—right here." The sharpie glided across the photograph, perpendicular to its center, intersecting other illustrative lines in its path. "Divide it into the passing millenniums and you get 9-1-1. September 11, 2001. The marking appeared on Myra three weeks before the World Trade Center attacks."

"Good God in heaven," the Monsignor gasped.

Dougherty put down another photograph of Myra's marking. "Scenario two, this picture was taken in November of 2004. The text here," Liam circled the important puzzle pieces. "Just below her shoulder, is in Aramaic, Jesus' true language. OMYBDW NYTMXTMW means…"

"Water," Hayden beat him to the punch.

"Sea. Angry sea."

"What are those Roman numerals?" the Monsignor asked.

"Coordinates. Longitude and latitude. Plug them into a global application and it pinpoints Indonesia. Sumatra, Indonesia to be more precise."

"The Tsunami," Monsignor shuttered. "Thousands perished."

"The marking appeared on Myra six weeks before the tidal wave struck the tiny island."

"Epochal insight," Hayden recognized. "She's…"

"Prophesying."

"And the third scenario, Liam?"

"Too early to tell. It's not over yet. There is another marking, more subtle, more discreet." Dougherty laid down yet another photo. "It is a hybrid of a Camargue Cross and a Triple Goddess…"

It was the very marking that Sister Marguerite discovered on the infant left on the church's door step on that faithful night, some nine years ago. The cross represented the three cardinal virtues of hope, faith, and charity. Or the three Marys of the New Testament. Mary, mother of Jesus. Mary, sister of Lazarus. And, of course, Mary Magdalene. The infant's bumpy impression that remained intact when a very confused Sister Marguerite ran her thumb over it was the Triple Goddess. Classical Greek lunar symbol depicting the three phases of the moon. Goddess of the dark, quiet and frightful. One who had her meals amid the graves? *Supreme Goddess of time and space…* The English poet John Skelton wrote of her…

Monsignor Hayden held up the photo, angling it for optimum light. "Mother of Gods. And men, and nature, mother of all things. Beginning and end are you, and you alone rule all. For things are from you, and in you doing all things, eternal one…comes to their end."

"The marking is a fusion of good and evil," Dougherty clarified.

"What is the significance?"

"Not sure," Dougherty admitted. "I do know this, to better understand the future, we have to know this child's past."

"Whatever you require, Liam. Take it as far as you like. This diocese is at your disposal."

"I'd also like to talk to her."

"Unfortunately, I'm afraid you'll find it a very one sided conversation." The Monsignor winced. "A lesson in futility."

"Maybe. But unless I miss my guess, she's been expecting me."

Dougherty walked into Myra's bedroom, squinting from the high-density blue lights. He paused and waited for his eyes to adjust. Myra ignored him at first. She sat at the foot of the bed, legs crossed under her, watching television. Dougherty approached the child, slowly, cautiously. "Hello Myra. I'm Liam. Unusual name, right? Easy way to remember, William shortened. My parents were lazy I guess. Can I sit a while?"

Myra gave Dougherty a quick once over, then her attention returned to the TV and the continuous high jinx of Timon and Pumbaa. Dougherty smoothly pulled up a chair and sat.

"The Lion King? A classic," he noted. "I'm partial to Toy Story. Had a toy cowboy growing up. Not as handsome as Woody. He was a raggedy old thing. But Butch was my best friend."

Silently and totally unexpectedly, Myra pulled out her doll from under her and proudly showed Dougherty.

"She's beautiful. What's her name?" There was an extended pause. Perhaps expecting a reply teetered on wishful thinking. It was, after all, exceeding early in their relationship to hope for a break through. But, then again, Dougherty didn't expect to meet Myra's doll. "It's OK. You don't have to tell me. Do you suppose if your doll met Butch, they would become friends?"

A half smile came to Myra slowly as the thought of it warmed her heart.

"Instant friends. I agree. Hey, did you know that the Lion King is on Broadway?" Myra's eyes widened with excitement. "Maybe we can talk Monsignor Hayden into giving us both time off for good behavior. I think I can score some tickets. They're hard to get, but I have friends in high places." Dougherty pointed up to heaven, sporting a goofy smirk. "I'll say a little prayer. Would you like to go?"

An ear-to-ear smile came to Myra quickly, stretching her petite features and amplifying her adorable dimples. It was an infectious grin that immediately illuminated the dreary, antiseptic ambience of institutional living. A loose front tooth suggested that a visit from the tooth fairy was in the child's near future. Anxious, Myra's pinky sprung up and she pointed it at Dougherty. She was requesting a customary pinkie swear. A visual contract, a moral lease, of sorts that relied exclusively on the honor system, rather than the courts. A pact, which if broken, would undoubtedly brand Dougherty as a big fat liar in the eyes of the child. Liam laughed as he wondered for a fleeting moment if he remembered how. It had been some time since anyone asked for that kind of commitment. Zelda Finklestein from his 8th grade class came to mind. She extended her pinkie, when Liam promised to call her for the dance. Dougherty and Myra locked pinkies. "I promise." Dougherty smiled. The commitment was made. For Liam, it was much like riding a bike, one never forgets how to pinky swear. "Well, nice to meet you Myra..." Dougherty extended his hand. Myra hesitated, and then shook it. "I'll get cracking on those tickets."

Dougherty slid the chair back in place and walked out. Myra began brushing her doll's hair.

In the quiet of the night, under the blanket of immunity the apartment offered, Dougherty confessed his thoughts to a tape recorder, a practice he instituted after he turned thirty and began to forget details. Dougherty conveniently blamed it on the aging process. It was far less than pinning his memory loss on the real felons, the booze and the drugs. Helplessly trapped in the throes of the natural progression of events, gave Liam the courage to face himself in the mirror.

"Dougherty Report, May 23 8:37 PM. Initial evaluation of Myra went well. I found her to be receptive, bright and animated. She's down right delightful. As expected Myra maintained her silence. Not certain at this point if it's a defense mechanism or something more deeply rooted?" Dougherty began doodling on his desk pad. "My concerns: Crigler-Najjar Syndrome. The child has surpassed her life expectancy. I promised to take her to a play. Her disorder requires that she remain under the blue lights for 12 hours a day. Maybe I can persuade Hayden to allow me to squeeze in a therapeutic night out. I hope so. It'll be tough to go back on a dying little girl's pinky swear…In summation, I reaffirm, to fully understand the enormity of the child's marking, it is imperative that we find Myra's roots. Track her origin. Friend or foe. Whatever we uncover, it is a necessary evil…" Dougherty depressed the recorder's button. He put down the microphone.

Arthur Shields appeared. "Why didn't you go on record with your other concerns? What if the kid's legit?"

"Go away, Artie," Dougherty sighed. "Not tonight."

"A true stigmata? What a hoot if you've been wrong all this time. Fess up, isn't that really your biggest concern, father?"

Dougherty began to tremble. He opened the top drawn of his desk and removed a pill bottle. Dougherty popped the Prozac and swallowed roughly as he squeezed his eyes shut. "Well, it should beeeee!" Arthur advised before fading from sight. Dougherty relished the silence. Arthur was gone. It was safe to open his eyes. As Liam waited for the medication to kick in, *timeline—uncomfortable numb in 17 minutes and counting*, he examined the latest photograph taken that very same day. In the picture, Sister Maria was bathing Myra. The child had her back to the camera. Her marking, referenced to as scenario three, was already more emphasized, populating more of Myra's freckled back. Also, in the nucleus of the imprint, the words, *HEAL THY* were definably etched under her skin.

CHAPTER THREE

Dougherty stood in line at the car rental place for nearly twenty minutes, but began formulating his complaints almost immediately. Patience was not one of his virtues evidenced by his incessant rehearsing, a plethora of suggestions each designed to improve the inept operation and make Cars for Less, a more efficient, customer friendly company. And oh yes, you could throw in eco conscious for good measure. When he finally made it up to the counter, Liam was too tired to voice a single complaint. And as for his dynamic suggestions, they could wait as well. After all, what does an ex-priest know about running a car rental business? Doreen, a college kid with a crooked nametag, greeted Dougherty. She input Liam's information into the system with the fastest fingers he had ever seen. The system in turn, spit out a two-page agreement. Doreen ripped it from the teeth of the printer, circled an item on each page with a loopy swirl and presented the contract to Dougherty.

"Just need you to initial the box and sign at the bottom, please," Doreen said mechanically.

"What kind of car is it?"

"It's the economy size."

"Economy?" he asked.

"Small."

"Well, how big is small?" Dougherty inquired deeper as he collected his papers.

"Fits two adults, two children and two bags comfortably." She fired off well practiced, accompanied by a fake smile just as polished. "Would you like to upgrade?"

With suitcase in hand and the mid day sun beating down on him, Dougherty lumbered through the white and red areas of the parking lot desperately searching for yellow 186. Savvy renters whizzed past him and effortlessly located their cars. Liam eventually stumbled into yellow, but the spots were in descending order. In spot 189 sat a spanking new convertible PT cruiser. Dougherty walked past 188, where a shinny Cadillac Escalade waited for some lucky renter. 187, a minted Cadillac DTS with alloyed wheels. Finally parked in 186, a maroon Chevrolet Aveo. *"Sweet,"* Dougherty thought. *"...Should have taken the upgrade."* Liam opened the trunk. He stuffed his suitcase in, repositioning it twice before he was able to close the trunk. Dougherty got in and started the car. Brake lights flared as he pulled out. His driving was a tad erratic. It was stop and go through the parking lot. The car lunged up to the security gate with a screech. The strapping security guard gave Dougherty a worrisome look as Liam opened the car window and handed him the paperwork.

"Sorry. I haven't driven in a while. I'm a little rusty."

"You going to be alright?" The guard asked looking over the contract.

"Fine. Just give me a hint, which one is the brake?" Dougherty laughed. The guard was not amused, in fact his look of concern intensified as he returned the paperwork.

"Kidding. I'm joking." Dougherty maintained as the giant arm on the gate slowly rose. "How do I get to the Pennsylvania Turnpike?"

"Map in the glove box." He answered without looking up from his back issue of Cosmopolitan. "Have a nice day."

Dougherty attempted to close the car window, but it got stuck in mid plight. Liam drove off with the same jerking motion.

By the time he found the Pennsylvania Turnpike, Dougherty found his groove. The Chevrolet hugged the right lane and traveled well under the speed limit as cars blew past him. Dougherty had both hands planted firmly on the steering wheel. A road map was opened and occupied the entire passenger seat. The map was upside down, crushed and folded in all the wrong spots. Dougherty couldn't make heads or tails of it His eyes darted from the road to the map, back to the road again as the car drifted into another lane. Car horns sounded. An exit crept up. At the last minute, Dougherty decided to take it, skidding on two wheels.

The Chevy coasted along the church's bumpy parking lot, kicking up dust and debris in its wake. Ultimately, the car slid into a spot and came to an abrupt halt. The door flew open and Dougherty spilled out of the cramped driver's seat. He rocked his torso back and fourth until his back ultimately cracked like an oversized walnut.

Dougherty walked into the church. He stood in the back and looked around the chapel. There were a few parishioners scattered about, some kneeling in prayer. Dougherty spotted a nun lighting a candle. "Excuse me, I'm looking for Sister Marguerite." He said softly as he approached her.

"You found her. And you are?"

"Dougherty. Liam Dougherty. We spoke on the phone."

"Of course, Father. We were expecting you this morning."

"I apologize. Got lost." Dougherty confessed. "Rand McNally I'm not. The only thing worse than my sense of direction is my driving. Hope I'm not too much of an inconvenience?"

"Not at all. Please let's sit," Sister Marguerite said leading him into the back pew.

"It's a lovely church."

"We like it. There are no bells and whistles in this house of worship, just a love of God. But I'm sure you didn't come to admire the simplicity or our architecture."

Dougherty shelved the pleasantries and got down to business. "I'd like to talk to you about the night of August 16, 2000. Do you recall that evening, Sister?"

"Its not every night you find a newborn on your door step."

"Thank goodness," Dougherty paused just long enough to take out a note pad. "May I take notes Sister?"

"Please," Sister Marguerite looked off as she tried to recall the details. "A lot of rain. A lot of wind. The storm shutters were banging around something fierce. It's a miracle we heard the knock at all..."

"I'm sorry," Dougherty interrupted. "We?"

"Sister Eleanor and myself. We were the only ones here."

"Is it possible we can ask Sister Eleanor to join us? Maybe she can add..."

The nun shook her head. "Sister Eleanor is no longer with us. Brain embolism. Poor dear never knew what hit her."

"My condolences."

"It'll be a year this fall." Sister Marguerite waved the sign of the cross.

"Anyhow, I opened the door and there stood this man. A figure in the night. He seemed to keep his distance. Careful not to come to close."

"What do you mean?"

The nun thought long and hard before answering. "He seemed—apprehensive."

"What did he look like?"

"Tall. Hooded. He was wearing a hood. I believe I saw his face, but strangely, I couldn't for the life of me, describe him. I couldn't that night for the police. And I still can't," Sister Marguerite stopped. It was obvious from her expressions that she had come to the unpleasant part of the recollection. The stranger had left her with a murky impression, shrouded with uncertainty. However she pressed on. "All I can say is that there was something about him, his presence—something very—" she stopped again. The nun was retelling the story bits and pieces at a time. It was as if she was dictating it to Dougherty in Morse code. The nun became frustrated. She could only imagine what Dougherty must have been thinking. Normally Sister Marguerite was as articulate as they come. But the events of that night tied her tongue, transforming her into a stuttering idiot. She finally threw in the towel. The nun simply smiled after a long struggle for words. "I don't know. I'm sorry."

"Well, it was a while ago…"

"Oh, I'll never forget the awe, the command about him."

Dougherty quickly jotted down notations. "Did he say anything, Sister?"

In her mind's eye, the nun conjured up Jonas' face. She could hear the howling wind as she focused in on his lips. And when Sister Marguerite repeated, "Take care of my little angel" for Dougherty, the nun heard the stranger's voice emanate from within her. Startled, she shrugged off the cold chill that raced up her spine.

"Maybe we should stop, Sister?"

"He was soft spoken, barely above a whisper," the nun continued. "I can't remember seeing his lips move. It all happened so quickly and in the chaos of the storm."

"Anything else about him? And please keep in mind Sister, any detail, no matter how minute, may be a terrific help."

The nun hesitated. Once again, in her mind's eye, she saw Jonas, turn away in slow motion. Thunder sounded. The stranger's red eyes flared against his hidden face hugging the eternal shadows.

"I thought I saw a flashing in his eyes."

"Flashing?"

"He left me with an overwhelming sense of urgency beyond my maternal instincts that the baby needed to be cared for, looked after. The stranger commissioned me. Unspoken, but I certainly understood. And I saw to it that child was placed into Saint Peters, the best orphanage this side of the Delaware Water Gap."

"How old was the baby?" Dougherty again put his pen to paper. "Best guess, days, weeks?"

"Hours. She was still covered in... well, the poor thing was a mess."

"What else can you tell me about the baby? Anything out of the ordinary?"

Sister Marguerite paused and searched. "Not that I can think of...oh, wait, she had a birth mark. She had been wrapped in a jacket. So I thought at first, the dye may have run or bled when the rain met fabric. But it would not wipe off. It would not budge. How is the child, Father?"

Dougherty smiled. "She is a delight. She is also gravely ill. Myra has a rare liver disorder. I'm trying to track down her parents for a more comprehensive medical history."

"Arduous task."

"Not quite the needle in the haystack. According to the CDC, out of the 100 or so cases of Crigler-Najjar worldwide, 20 percent are among the Amish in Pennsylvania."

"Lancaster is a county over. Not far. Have you contacted the local police?"

"Cops have nothing. They have been no help."

Sister Marguerite was more disappointed than surprised. "The Amish are a very tight lipped community." The nun sighed, than fired point blank, "forgive me for asking Father, but why would the Archdiocese of Trenton send a clergymen to find a child's parents?"

Dougherty smirked at the nun's astuteness. However, Liam dismissed any obligation he may have felt to answer her. It was exceeding early in his investigation, and some things were wiser left unsaid. Dougherty stood up and jammed his notes into his back pocket.

"Thank you for your time, Sister. You've been very helpful." He shook her hand. "And again, I'm sorry for your loss." Dougherty not only sidestepped his way out of an awkward reply, but also out of the pew. He marched out of the church with far more questions than he had hoped.

Lucky's Inn and BBQ Pit was a no star accommodation that made the Bates Motel look like the Four Seasons. Sandwiched between Lincoln Highway and a creek, the sleazy, short stay pigpen was a den of iniquity of biblical proportions. On an architectural note, the motel was a disenfranchised mortar and failing neon. Aesthetically, the grounds needed work, a great deal of work. The motel's curb appeal was a deterrent, boasting unevenly landscaped shrubbery and a rose garden littered with spent condoms. In all its charm and splendor, Lucky's was home to young people looking to quench their raging hormones. And for the young at heart, the motel represented the Viagara Falls of Lancaster, PA.

Dougherty's car sat outside room 21 in a half assed vertical parking job that took up two spots. Liam hadn't quite gotten the knack of the all-important "park", but he was progressing by leaps and bounds.

Room 21 offered no surprises. It was everything you'd expect for $39.99 and less. It was dark, dingy, and degrading. Soundless, except for the intermittent buzz of the neon bulbs in the broken motel sign. The furnishings were sparse, a filthy mirror with the impassioned plea, *Clean Me* written in grime. An antique dresser with a 19-inch Zenith angled toward a ratty powder blue rocker. On top of the television, there was a contraption that dispensed free HBO. Dougherty set up shop on the uneven nightstand. His Toshiba laptop with its air card pointed east for optimum reception. He sat on the side of the bed, on top of the stained bedspread ever mindful of any potential love puddles that housekeeping may have over looked. Google populated his computer screen as Dougherty typed in *Obstetrics and Gynecology – Lancaster, Pennsylvania.* The search instantaneously returned the local business results, names,

addresses and telephone numbers. Dougherty narrowed the
hunt by opening a road map and circling addresses within a
five-mile radius of the Amish community. His trusty black
sharpie had seen better days. Its ink was drying up and the tip
had become down right bumpy, but the marker still managed to
highlight the area from Manor Ridge to East Lampster and
from Millerville to just past the Lancaster Country Club.
Dougherty removed his cell phone and began dialing. The
room silence was pieced by the sound of a headboard knocking
against the opposite wall with moans quickly following.
Although difficult, Dougherty ignored the sounds of sex, and
concentrated on the business at hand.

"Yes, hello…," he said into the phone. "May I speak to
Doctor Laszlo please? No. I'm not a patient. My name is Liam
Dougherty. I'm with the Archdiocese in Trenton, New
Jersey…"

And so it began. Dougherty paced, making his phone calls
for the better part of the day. He spoke to physicians, recep-
tionists, and answering machines a like, neither wheeled any
quantitative results. The conversations were capricious at best.
There seemed to be an underlying hesitance to commit. For
Dougherty, the only constant was the headboard pounding
against the long wall. The events of the day were beginning to
take its toll. He walked into the bathroom and splashed cold

water on his face with his cell phone glued to his ear. "...Of course Doctor Neuwirth. I am well aware of the patient's privacy act. But a little girl is dying..." Suddenly there was a click. "...Hello? Hello..." Dougherty realized that the good doctor had hung up on him. "Son-of-a...." Liam marched out of the bathroom and over the night table. Where a list of physicians sat defaced in all directions with various notations, reminders and just plain doodling. Dougherty crossed out Doctor Neuwirth with a vengeance. Suddenly, Liam's cell phone rang. He quickly answered before collapsing onto the bed. "Yes Doctor Ziegler. Thank you for returning my call. My patient is a nine-year-old female. She suffers from Crigler-Najjar Syndrome. She's on the donor list, yes. No. I haven't got a clue. As I mentioned, she was brought to a church shortly after her birth. My guess, they were an Amish couple. Sure. Do you have a pen? Liam Dougherty. That's D-O-U-G-H-E-R-T-Y. The contact person in Trenton is Monsignor Hydan at 609 555-3371. And you have my number. Feel free anytime day or night. Thank you so much doctor."

Dougherty hung up. *Finally, movement—a potential break in the case*. He thought as he rubbed the frustration off his face and sighed. Once again, moans interrupted the relative quiet. More headboard action. It sounded like Alex Van Halen was in the next room. Dougherty surrendered to an incredulous smile. He could do nothing more than close his eyes and enjoy the drum solo.

An exquisitely good-looking day. Sun drenched acres upon rolling acres of crisp green countryside as far as the eye could see, under an umbrella of endless blue skies. Dougherty's car puttered and coughed until it came to Doctor Ziegler's white farmhouse at the end of a twisting dirt road. The Chevy parked next to a horse and buggy. Liam got out of the car and stared at the primitive, single horse-powered means of transportation. Dougherty was so fascinated; the quintessential city boy seized the opportunity to pet the animal. Long strokes under its harness that seemed to please both the horse and Dougherty alike. The closest he had ever been to a horse was standing at the finish line at Monmouth racetrack. But touching, feeling the powerful, yet remarkably docile steed was another story entirely.

Dougherty walked into the Doctor's office and announced himself to the receptionist. Liam proceeded to the waiting area and sat across from an Amish couple. The gentleman was dressed traditionally, plain pale shirt with a shoulder banded collar. His dark suspenders contrasted greatly, giving him an almost 3-D effect. The gentleman's dark pants crept up in the sitting position, revealing ankle-high black leather shoes. The attire was accented with a straw hat that matched nothing. His wife was also clad conventionally, in a dark cape dress with a pleated waist, matching belt and a round headdress tucked neatly behind her ears. She also sported black high top shoes with laces.

"William...," the receptionist called.

"Liam," Dougherty corrected her as he stood up.

"Doctor Ziegler will see you now."

As Dougherty walked past the reception area, another Amish woman exited one of the examining rooms. He smiled at her. The woman's eyes submissively dropped down. She deliberately turned away from Dougherty, careful not to make eye contact with an outsider. Liam continued on into the empty consultation room. Doctor Ziegler followed him in, holding a folder under his arm. The doctor was in his 50's, stocky with a bad toupee. Ziegler looked more like a boxer, a junior lightweight, than a man of medicine.

"Thank you for seeing me, doctor," the men exchanged handshakes.

"Not at all. Sit, Father. Please," the doctor sat behind his desk and in front of a wall of medical degrees as well as 8 X 10's of his most recent fishing triumphs. An extended look revealed Ziegler, in a full fisherman out fit posing proudly next to a 25-pound Tuna, his prize Swordfish and a giant lobster, respectively. Dougherty took a seat across from him. "By the way, Monsignor Hayden wants you to call him."

"Thank you. I will," Liam noted.

"We got lucky." Ziegler tossed Dougherty the folder. "We usually archive our inactive files. Records three years or older, could sometimes take up to a week to retrieve. But Lola remembered the patient. Payne. Anna Payne. Husband, Jonas."

Dougherty glanced through the file. "Now why would your receptionist remember her?" Liam asked. "It was nine years ago. I'm sure you've seen hundreds of expectant mothers since."

"You're right. I don't remember what I had for breakfast this morning. But the Paynes, for an Amish couple, were a little more hip. More modernized. Worldly. Mrs. Payne had a sense of humor which is rare in these parts."

"Anything out of the ordinary about the pregnancy?"

The Doctor nodded. "She was 34 weeks last time I saw her. I saw her in early August 2000. Mrs. Payne simply stopped coming...missed a few appointments."

"Did you try phoning her?"

"The Amish don't have telephones, Father. They believe it brings in the outside world. They're right," Ziegler paused. "No, our office assumed that the Paynes had a change of heart and went with a more traditional birth, a mid wife. It's not uncommon."

"Ever meet Mr. Payne?"

"On several occasions. Soft spoken. Very involved with the pregnancy. Aside from that, there's very little else I can recall. There's an address in the file. But keep in mind, it's nine years old."

"Thank you so much for your time, Doctor."

"I hope it helps the little girl."

"Would you mind if I asked your receptionist—uh—uh—"

"Lola."

"Yes. Lola. Sorry. Can I ask her a few questions?"

"She's the real brain of this operation. But proceed with caution, the closer it gets to quitting time, the crankier Lola becomes."

Dougherty laughed. "Thanks for the tip."

Dougherty walked out of the farmhouse and began dialing his cell phone. Liam stood outside his car and once again caressed the horse; doubtful he would ever get another chance. "Monsignor Hayden, please. Thanks," he said into the phone. "Charles, Liam, my phone needs charging so if I lose you, I'll call you back when I get back to the motel. How's our girl? Really? Are you certain? Can you email it to me? Send it as an

attachment. I'd like to get started decomposing it immediately
—Charles? Charles, are you there?"

The cell phone turned off with a beep. Dougherty got in
his car and drove off.

CHAPTER FOUR

Dougherty doubled back to Lucky's Inn and BBQ Pit, before embarking on his final and most important destination. Liam sat on the bed and powered up his laptop. Scattered across the bed was Anna Payne's file as well as hamburger wrappers and an empty bag of McDonalds. He opened the Monsignor's email marked *URGENT* and downloaded the attachment. Myra's marking populated the screen and Dougherty got busy deciphering it, periodically taking a break long enough to stuff a golden brown French fry into his mouth. It appeared that the Monsignor was correct. The child's third scenario was complete. Dougherty input some data and the marking shifted to the right. Liam cross-referenced Myra's imprint with streaming data on the left. An instant match was highlighted and segregated for further analysis. Similar patterns indicated to Dougherty that like its predecessors, the marking was not written in past or present. It was, indeed, another glimpse into the future. His preliminary findings were so astounding, so significant that their implications for Catholicism and the rest of the world frightened him. Of course, his inferences would require more scrutiny before Liam could present them to the governing body at Trenton, namely Bishop Terrence. Dougherty was greatly concerned that the last portion on the scenario was faint, barely legible. That suggested that the child was weakening and Myra's health was deteriorating.

So much was riding on his visit to the Paynes. If Dougherty actual believed in God, he would have prayed that the visit would be productive and not another dead end. The million-dollar question, would the Paynes open up to him about what must have been a dark chapter in their lives? In the horse-drawn community, Dougherty was not exactly perceived as William Penn. But Liam was hoping that their paternal instincts would prevail.

With his trusty road map, once again, out stretched across the passenger seat and the address to the Payne's place on a sticky pad, posted on the dashboard, Dougherty's Chevy continued to navigate along the back roads to nowhere. Liam's eyes drifted up from the map. He immediately slammed on the brakes. The car skidded to a complete stop just as the road ended and the tall weeds began. Everything in the car shifted and bounced wildly. *How can a road just dead end without warning?* Liam wondered, missing the simplicity of the Garden State Parkway, or the predictability of Route 9. Dougherty wasn't in New Jersey, and getting use to the notion was going to take a little time. When Dougherty regained composure, he jammed the car into reverse and executed a clumsy, K turn. A dust cloud swallowed the car as it fishtailed back down the road until it came to a turn off. Dougherty took a hard right on to the bumpy cut-through.

The Chevy recklessly bounced; as it mowed down patches of tall weeds. Weird noises billowed out from its undercarriage, a high-pitched howl as if someone was choking a small barnyard animal. The car's bumper scrapped the curb, before spilling out behind a filling station and an adjunct strip of stores. It was high time that Dougherty admitted the obvious, he was certainly lost. In his forehead, the General Store appeared to him like a beacon, a messenger from the lord—a burning bush. So like any clueless traveler, he got out to stretch his legs. And if the store proved not to be divine intervention, at the very least, Liam could wet his parched whistle with a cold diet anything.

Dougherty walked into the General Store and went directly over to the freezer. He withdrew a soda and brought it up to the counter, where Earl Holander, the proprietor was waiting. Earl was in his 70's. He was wearing a flannel shirt and overalls. An Amish boy, no more than 10 years old was playing handball against the counter. The boy was dressed in traditional Amish attire.

"What can I do ya for?" Earl asked in a redneck, I-just-married-my-sister, accent.

Dougherty put the bottle down and handed Earl money. "Hoping for some directions." Dougherty read off the post it. "731 Oakdale trail?"

The store had an over abundance of country décor and Earl's old relic of a cash register was no exception. As Earl Rang in the sale, the numbers 8-0 immediately popped up. The digits were yellow with age and, like Earl, had seen better days. Earl scooped up Dougherty's change and stopped to think. "7-3-1 Oakdale...?

"Maybe you know them, the Paynes?"

The boy immediately stopped bouncing the ball. He became uncomfortable as he re-directed his attention to Dougherty.

"Nobody goes to "pagan" Paynes' place," the boy said in a spooked tone. "Noooobody."

"Why do you call him "pagan" Payne, little buddy?" Dougherty asked.

Before the boy could answer, his mother grabbed him from behind and rushed him down the aisle away from Liam. In an angry voice, she scolded the boy in a German dialect spoken only among the Amish. The woman shoved the boy toward the door. More German. The boy walked out of the store. The woman ducked down another aisle and resumed shopping.

"Jonas' place," Earl fessed up. "We deliver to him every Friday." The proprietor stepped out from the counter, real neighbor-like and pointed out the door with yellow tobacco stained fingers. "What you're going to want to do is drive out here and hang a right, continue on 516 until you come to an abandon drive in. That's Oakdale Trail. From there just follow the numbers."

Dougherty thanked Earl and walked out of the General store, unwrapping a piece of Bazooka. He read the Bazooka Joe comic and smiled. The Amish boy was throwing his ball against the side of the house.

"Hey, little buddy…" Initially, the Amish boy ignored Dougherty. "Want some gum? Grape flavored." Liam unscrupulously tempted the young lad like that silver-tongued serpent from the Garden of Eden fame. For an unflattering moment, Dougherty had displayed the cunning charms; he used to illustrate the perils of allurement. Liam simply replaced the forbidden fruit with a harmless piece of Bazooka.

The boy shrugged with indifference, but his eyes said it all as they widened with excitement. Dougherty tosses him the gum. The boy quickly unwrapped it and jammed it into his mouth.

"So, what did you mean by "Pagan" Payne?" Dougherty persisted, knowing full well that the boy would have signed over his soul after that grape flavored explosion. The boy knew that if he played his cards right, and said all the right things; he could very well be tastefully rewarded a second time.

"Ma says he's a sinner. He doesn't belong anymore."

"Why?" Dougherty scratched his head. "What did he do?"

The screen door slammed. The Amish woman bolted out of the store with groceries. More German dialect from the woman. She grabbed her son's arm and forced him to remove the gum. The woman pulled the boy away.

"Have a nice day," Dougherty offered in an effort to quench any hard feelings.

Jonas Paynes' farmhouse was plain and modest. A two story white colonial with green shutters, nestled on top of a hill with an 1803 stone bank barn adjacent to it. In the barn and the surrounding meadows, goats, sheep, cows and chickens were frolicking about. The entire property was fenced off. Its massive gate was closed. The sprawling driveway was also off limits. Dougherty was forced to park his car at the side of the road. He got out and looked at Jonas Payne in the distance. Jonas was working on his horse drawn plow with his back to Dougherty. Liam tried to open the gate, but it was locked. He quickly, discreetly hopped the fence. As Dougherty's Bruno Maglias touched down on Payne's property, Jonas' eyes widened. He stopped prepping his plow and looked up, sensing the priest on his land. Jonas had not lost his rugged good looks, although, he appeared raggy, unkempt. The once jet-black shoulder length hair was now streaked with gray. His scruffy beard, also gray in spots. Jonas' dark eyes were tired and filled with disappointment. His dress, a scaled down version of Amish attire. Mr. Payne's muscular torso challenged the seams of his soiled pale shirt with every move he made. His sleeves were rolled up, exposing his thick forearms. Dougherty walked up to him. Jonas kept his back to Liam.

"You're trespassing, mister." Jonas said.

"I'm looking for Mr. Payne."

"I said you're trespassing."

"I'm Father Dougherty," Liam announced as Jonas' face mildly contorted. "I work with the Archdiocese of Trenton, New Jersey…"

"Mister, do I need to call the law?" Jonas engaged the plow. Dougherty noticed a birthmark of sorts. A dark circle with a half moon seated on top. It was the *Camargue Cross* and the *Triple Goddess*. They were remarkably similar to Myra's birthmark.

"I can see you're busy, I'll keep it brief. The date August 16, 2000, ring a bell? It was the day your daughter was born. It just so happens it was the same day a newborn was dropped off at the church of the Blessed Mother in Strasburg. It was your child was it not?"

"I don't know what you're talking about."

"Perhaps Mrs. Payne will remember. Is she available?" Dougherty turned toward the house, shielding his eyes from the sun's glare.

"Look mister…" Jonas attempted to remain civil.

"Your child is ill. Seriously ill. We need to get some answers or she will not survive. Can I be any clearer?"

"Good day, Mr. Dougherty."

"Your daughter is going to die," Dougherty said forcefully, pulling no punches. "Don't abandon her again."

Jonas attempted to climb on to the plow. "Don't walk away from me. I'm talking to you." Frustrated, Dougherty grabbed Jonas' arm. The farmer's eyes once again widened. He winced, anticipating pain from his contact with the alleged man of God. Jonas paused and stared at Dougherty's hand. There was no pain. Not the slightest twinge of discomfort.

"You're no priest," Jonas said, looking through Dougherty while pulling his arm back. "Now leave!!!"

Jonas leaped onto his plow and rode off to tend to his corn crop. Dougherty was left standing alone, contemplating his next move. Suddenly, a bible scripture flooded through Liam; it was Revelations chapter 20 verses 1 and 2. "…And I saw an *angel coming down out of heaven with the key to the abyss and a great chain in his hand. And he seized the dragon, the original serpent, who is the devil and Satan and bound him for a thousand years. And he hurled him into the abyss and shut it and sealed it over him that he might not mislead the nations anymore…"*

It was a passage that had remained vague and dubious since John the Elder wrote it in 96 C.E. in Asia Minor. Unclear until now. Catholicism had maintained throughout the ages that although the King James Version of the bible ended with the book of Revelation, it was not the final chapter of God's word. There were simply too many loose ends. Unanswered questions. Namely and most importantly, how do we hurl Satan into the abyss?

The conference room at the Trenton Archdiocese was long, antiseptic—void of emotion and echoic. Dougherty stood at the podium, attempting to convey what he believed, what he knew in his heart to be true. He was surprisingly composed as he presented his finding to the elders of the diocese. In attendance, at the round table, were Bishop Terrence, Monsignors Hayden and McElroy, Fathers Cobb, Clemens and Edwards. Also present, but not a member of the governing body was Deacon Izzo, who took notes as a matter of record.

With remote in hand, Dougherty turned on the overhead slide projection with a click. Myra's markings filled the blank screen. There were some rumbling from the group.

"I hope everyone had an opportunity to review my report and are familiar with Myra and her unique gift," Dougherty began, clearing his throat. "The child's marking, her third scenario, if you will, now offers us the possibility that the bible's final chapter may actually exist. The lost book is called Terminus. From the Latin word *Terminatio* or the end."

"How do we know it isn't a chapter omitted from the middle of the bible?" Monsignor McElroy interrupted.

Dougherty aimed from laser pointer at a section of the child's marking. "Inverted symbols of Genesis, the first book of the bible," Liam explained. "Inverted symbols denote opposite or contradictory. Genesis/beginning. Terminus/End. Perfectly book ended. I believe Terminus had to be penned by John the Elder as well. I arrive at that theory by process of elimination. There weren't many qualified at the time to put pen to paper. I believe it to have been completed in 99 C.E. Then it suddenly and mysteriously disappeared."

Father Cobb raised his hand before calling out. "Father Dougherty, I submit to you, does Terminus even matter at this stage of the game?"

"Well, if we question its relevance ask yourself, out of 66 books that made it into the bible, why did Terminus simply vanish? Who had the most to gain by its exclusion?" Dougherty said.

"But where on earth is it and how do we retrieve it?" Father Clemens asked.

"Romania," Dougherty fired back without flinching.

"How do we know that? We can't be certain," Father Clemens continued his campaign of skepticism.

Once again, Liam enlisted the aid of his pointer. "The markings, Latitude 46.78 degrees north. Longitude 23.59 degrees east…"

Dougherty changed the slide. A world map splashed across the screen. Latitude and longitude crossed. The coordinates highlighted Romania.

"Romania, then what?" Father McElroy asked. Surely there are dozens of counties, towns and communes throughout the country."

"Needle in a haystack," Father Edwards chimed in.

The slide changed back to Myra's marking.

"This final grouping of numbers," Dougherty emphasized. "…2803 matches the exact population of Cluj."

The Bishop Terrence sunk deeper into his leather chair. The Bishop paused as he wrestled with the preponderance of evidence. "In dissecting the little girls alleged prophecy with your high tech scalps, you're left with not much more than speculation and conjuncture."

"The child has not been wrong yet," Dougherty confirmed.

"Still, it remains merely a hunch," the bishop insisted.

The bureaucracy was beginning to irritate Dougherty, like jock itch on a hot summer day. "Make no mistake about it your Excellency, Terminus is in Cluj, Romania. And with all due respect to this governing body, I'm going regardless of your endorsement."

"Duly noted," Terrence nodded, unsure of a proper reply.

Monsignor Hayden wasn't taking any chances. He had seen these impartial hearings spiral out of control. The governing body was a finicky bunch, steeped in old fashion tradition where disrespect came with its own veto power. Hayden leaped out of his seat. "At this time, this committee would like to thank Father Dougherty for his tireless and selfless efforts in this case. It is quite apparent that he is passionate about the work at hand."

"Father Dougherty, will you give us a moment?" Bishop Terrence requested.

"Certainly," Dougherty agreed as he stepped away from the podium and walked out of the room. Bishop Terrence looked at Myra's larger than life projected marking on the screen. He took a moment to ingest it, and then turned to Monsignor Hayden. "Tell me, is he still drinking?"

Dougherty paced the marble corridor of the divinity, before sitting on a wooden bench outside the conference room. Banished to the hallway, Liam felt like a mischievous high school sophomore waiting punishment to be handed down by the dean. What the governing body didn't get was that time was of the essence. There simply wasn't room for red tape. Myra's life hung in the balance. Every rotation of the preverbal second hand, the child was that much closer to drawing her final breath.

Minutes felt like hours, as Dougherty remained hopelessly optimistic, but handcuffed and suspended in time in the throes of a decision. He did a mental reconciliation of his checkbook. Who was he kidding? Dougherty couldn't finance a trip to the Philadelphia Zoo much less airfare to Romania. His grand soapbox gesture, vowing to pursue Terminus with or without the support of the diocese was a bluff. Dougherty was hoping that Bishop Terrence could not see beyond his poker face. The conference room's heavy Oak doors opened with a resounding echo, as did Monsignor Hayden's approaching footsteps.

"That was one hell of a compelling homily Liam," Hayden nodded. "When can you leave?"

The diocese had spoken. It was official. Dougherty would leave for Romania immediately. But Liam had some unfinished business.

Dougherty quietly walked into Myra's bedroom. Again, he squinted until his eyes adjusted to the blue lights. Myra was in bed. Liam walked close and saw that she was sleeping soundly. He didn't want to wake her. Dougherty took a minute to review her medical chart. The child's vital signs were stable, for the moment. He removed a pair of tickets from the inside pocket of his sport jacket and placed them on the night table. Myra stirred. She listlessly opened her eyes and smiled at Dougherty.

"How's my favorite girl?" Dougherty smiled back. "Sorry. I didn't mean to wake you. But I'm glad you're up." Liam waved the tickets. Myra's bloodshot eyes welled up with excitement. "I sold the night out to the Monsignor. Sister Maria will be joining us. Anyhow, 3rd row the Lion King next month. Be there or be square."

Myra picked the tickets off the night table and stared at them.

"Myra, I have to go on a trip, a business trip. I may not see you for a while. So take care of yourself. Get some rest. Get plenty of rest…" Dougherty leaned over and kissed her forehead. He turned to walk away, the child grabbed his arm.

"Don't go!" Myra said in the sweetest angel voice, as traces of a smile were gone.

Surprised, Dougherty looked at her. "What?" he asked. Dougherty heard her perfectly fine the first time; he just wanted to hear her talk.

"I don't want you to go!"

Dougherty could not hide his delight. "You spoke. You spoke to me. I'm honored."

"Please don't go!" She repeated.

"Why Myra? Why shouldn't I go?"

"It could be bad. I'm scared."

"Why are you scared?"

"The darkness," Myra warned as the drowsiness returned. "Don't go!"

"What darkness? Myra, what about the darkness?"

"I'm tired now." Myra's pretty little voice tailed off.

Myra fell asleep clutching the tickets. Dougherty continued to stare at her.

Planes roared overhead at Newark International Airport. Cars were darting in and out of lanes, unloading passengers at the departure terminal. Port Authority police were trying to maintain some semblance of traffic flow. A dark sedan pulled up in front of terminal B. Its doors flew open. Father Leonard, in full clergy attire, rushed around to the back of the car. Dougherty climbed out of the passenger side and removed a duffle bag from the back seat. Father Leonard wrestled with Liam's over stuffed suitcase, before yanking it out of the trunk. Leonard carried the luggage over to the curb where he was met by a police officer.

"Move it!" the cop barked.

"It's OK," Father Leonard said. "I won't be long."

"I said move that car!!!"

Father Leonard ignored the officer. "Peace be with you, Father Dougherty."

"And also with you." Liam looked at the officer's nametag. It read: *Rabinowitz*. Dougherty smiled. "You're going to need it."

"Alright that's it." The police officer removed a summons pad from his back pocket. "Let me see your license and registration!!!"

As Father Leonard thumbed through his wallet, Dougherty walked into the terminal with his suitcase in hand and faded into the crush of travelers.

The bird's eye view from the roof of the Archdiocese was invigorating.   The nocturnal urban backdrop provided a false sense of tranquility, in crisp, panoramic surrealism.   The lights of Trenton twinkled below as a transient hush fell on a vibrant downtown at rest.   Clouds raced across the half moon, undermining its glow and giving way to shadowy after thoughts of things to come.   Ever mindful that Dougherty's wing tip was somewhere over the North Atlantic, out of nowhere, as if the sky opened up like a flash, Jonas Payne landed on the roof with a thud.   Instantly, his face contorted from the pain as Jonas' feet began to burn when he made contact with the hallowed ground. The smoldering soles of his shoes liquefied and melted onto the black top in a spreading puddle of molten rubber.   Jonas ignored the agony of his blistering bare feet.   He cocked his fist, muscles bulged through his shirt.   His abs rippled across his stomach, in small waves of descending might as he punched a hole through the roof.   Jonas quickly tore away at the asphalt and effortlessly peeled back the metal ductwork as if he were skinning a banana.   All the while his hands were smoking. Ambers of his singed flesh floated upward toward the heavens like tiny radiant souls en route to their clandestine rendezvous with St. Peter.

Inside the Trenton Archdiocese, in Monsignor Hayden's living quarters, the monsignor was asleep. He was lying in bed motionless, wearing a contoured eye mask. Frantic knocking ensued. Hayden stirred. The knocking quickly turned to pounding. The monsignor sprung up from bed. Disoriented at first, he removed the mask and fumbled around the night table for his glasses.

"Monsignor Hayden, please sir, its urgent." Sister Marie called out over the frenzied knocking.

The Monsignor staggered out of bed in his nightshirt and opened the door. "Yes…"

Sister Marie was panic stricken and on the verge of tears. "Sorry to bother you sir," she said interrupted by a series of sobs.

"Not at all. What is it Sister?"

Sister Marie ushered the Monsignor into Myra's bedroom. The metal door had been ripped off its hinges and folded in two as if it were a piece of loose-leaf paper. Myra was gone.

"Call the police, Sister!" In a residual state of shock, the nun simply stared off and sobbed. "Do it NOW, Sister Marie!!!!

The nun scampered off. Monsignor Hayden's look of concern intensified as he stared at the child's empty bed.

CHAPTER FIVE

There was a significant police presence snooping around the entire diocese all morning and well into the afternoon. The east wing stairwell was completely cordoned off. Monsignor Hayden, assisted detectives Baker and Simms with their investigation. Both detectives, in their early 40's were causally dressed, but neat. What they had on their hands besides a missing girl was a crime scene that defied rationale. They stared with disbelief at the gaping hole in the roof. Beyond the crushed steel, beyond the ripped metal and beyond logic, the cops saw only daylight and blue skies through the perforated opening. If you break down the facts to their barest components and strip away any preconceived notions, nothing made sense. It wasn't the detectives first day on the job. In fact, collectively, they had nearly 45 years of police work under their belt, yet this was new for both of them. Maybe even the whole damn Trenton police force.

"…Half inch thick steel," Detective Baker was thinking out loud. "Looks like a chunk of the header is missing…"

"What the hell could have caused that?" Detective Simms caught himself. "Excuse me, father."

"Nothing short of a jack hammer." Baker turned to the monsignor. "And no one heard anything?"

"No sir."

"Impossible," Simms snapped. "It would have been the equivalent of someone driving a freight train through your living room while you napped on the recliner."

"Ask for yourself," the Monsignor offered.

"We intend to," Simms said.

"Again, my concern is for the child's health. She requires special care without it she will surely perish."

"We are not going to let that happen." Detective Baker assured the Monsignor. "An Amber alert is already in effect. The feds are on their way. The little girl will turn up."

"How long do we have Monsignor?" Simms asked.

"Hard to say. Nine, maybe ten hours before her organs begin shutting down."

By the middle of the afternoon, as a humidity-induced haze hung over the city, the investigation heated up. Federal Agents Biggers and Doleman, dark suits, darker shades had taken over the case. They blanketed the roof looking for clues that local law enforcement might have overlooked. The agents inspect the hole with its twisted steel and mangled ductwork. Biggers noticed a charred stain next to the opening. It was the remains of Jonas' shoe that melted into the asphalt upon contact. The blotch didn't belong. The agent poked at it with a pen. It felt foreign. Biggers sniffed the pen for residue. But it was not immediately recognizable to the agent. "We should get a sample of this," Biggers said to Doleman. "Maybe we'll get lucky."

Detective Baker, once a fed wannabe stood behind the agents and took mental notes. Simms combed the roof perimeter for the umpteenth time. Monsignor Hayden paced in the background.

"Any surveillance cameras?" Agent Biggers asked.

The Monsignor sullenly nodded. "A requisition request has been on the Bishop's desk since 07."

Agent Bigger turned to his partner. "Let's check the surrounding roof tops for video. Maybe we'll get lucky as well."

"The child is ill," Monsignor Hayden reiterated. "Extreme-ly ill."

"We know," Biggers said. "We're going to do everything we can Monsignor."

"And of course, anything you need, you have the full support of this diocese."

Agent Doleman panned the rooftop. "I don't get it. Once you're up here, then what? The only place to go is—"

Simms peeked over the edge at the 14-story plunge onto a crowed East State Street below. "Down." The detective shrugged as a police helicopter hover over them.

An explosion of law enforcement shattered the tranquility
of the Amish community as Jonas Payne's farmhouse was
besieged by a whirlwind of police activity. Patrol cars, some
marked, others not, converged on the scene. Their doors flew
open and officers with their guns drawn, fanned out across
Pagan Payne's place. Within seconds, Pennsylvania State and
local authorities surrounded the peaceful farmhouse. Jonas'
neighbors were in the fields working their crop. They heard the
sound of approaching helicopters, and looked up to watch the
spectacle. The harsh reality of the real world crashing into
theirs as the shadow of the choppers streaked across the fertile
fields. One helicopter touched down yards from the
farmhouse. The other remained hovering about, providing
tactical air support should it become necessary. Agents Biggers
and Doleman hopped out of the helicopter and helped
Monsignor Hayden out of the chopper, battling the gusty winds
created by the swirling propeller. They walked to the farmhouse
and proceeded up the front porch, where they are met by a rush
of officers from the Lancaster County Police Department.
Biggers knocked. No reply. He knocked again. Nothing. The
agent motioned to a State Trooper. Out came the battering ram
and down went the door. The force split the door unevenly,
showering the charging first responders with splintered debris as
the cops flooded the place. They raced down the narrow

hallway and branched off into the various rooms with their assault rifles at the ready. The Feds and Monsignor Hayden remained in the front of the house. The furnishings were sparse and unpretentious. Such was the Amish way of life. In the kitchen there was a wood-burning stove, a table with a bowl of fruit on top, accompanied by four plain chairs. Its cushions were worn with a checkered pattern. The living room had even fewer material possessions, a sofa and rocking chair. It was a typical Amish household with one blaring exception, the walls were covered, floor to ceiling with photographs of Anna Payne. The pictures, some color, others black and white in various sizes were literally plastered over every inch of available wall space. It was a make shift shrine to Anna in thousands of Kodak moments, a testament to their joyous life together.

The Federal agents gawked with perplexity, ingesting Jonas' obsession. Quite possibly his disease. Every cop that passed stopped and stared. Even Monsignor Hayden was baffled and offered no immediate explanation. The police filed out of the back rooms.

"Nothing. Place is clean," a State Trooper offered up as the oddity of the walls captured his undivided attention.

"This guy is definitely—" the monsignor stuttered, unable to take his eyes off the bizarre montage.

"A person of interest…," Biggers confirmed.

Point Pleasant was a quiet and picturesque fishing village. So it was no surprise that visitors of the Garden State seemed to have the quaint little town on their things to see list. Barnegat Bay Marina, along with other amenities, presented tourists and locals alike the opportunity to bond with the sea. Surrounded on all sides by a choppy Atlantic, most of the slips were empty. Boats that were docked were bouncing into the pier in the wake of splashing water. Sea gulls offered an overture of squawking as they landed and took off at will. Captain Jack's Charters, was located at the beginning of the pier, adjunct to Captain Jack's Bait & Tackle across from Captain Jack's Gas for Less. In the window of the dilapidated shack, next to a hand written sign that read; *Rentals by the hour, by the day…* Captain Jack in the flesh peeked out. Captain Jack looked more like the Gloucester fishermen, than a thriving entrepreneur. He sat next to the window reading Playboy and listening to the radio. "*…Dow is down 85 points on disappointing housing data,*" 104.4, the Jersey shore's all news, all the time, reported. "*…Nasdaq and S&P 500 down fractionally. In Trenton this morning, a brazen kidnapping and police are asking for your help. A young girl was…*(static)*…. her bedroom…*(static)"

Suddenly there was less news and more static. Its signal scrambled and "all news, all the time" bled into "sounds of the 70's." The new station flickered as Elton John's "Island Girl" filled the airwaves. The song however continued to fade in and out. First, bashfully above a whisper, then suddenly, blaring as if amplified through a bullhorn. Captain Jack whacked at the radio with an open fist. No change. Something was wreaking havoc with the frequency. Jonas appeared in the window, startling the Captain.

"Scared the bejesus out of me," Jack grabbed his chest, half joking. "What can I do for you, young man?"

"I need a boat."

"Sorry all our leisure boats are rented."

Jonas pointed to a 48 foot Sea Ray 480. "What about that one?"

"The Nuwave? That's my baby. Going out for blues in an hour."

"I'll take it."

"Oh, I couldn't possibly…"

Jonas locked stares with the Captain. Once Jack was mentally impaled, Jonas momentarily suspended his inalienable right to free will. And then, Mr. Payne went to work, telepathically re-asserting his request using a command a tad more potent than the power of suggestion.

"You can! And you will!" Jonas nodded.

"I can. I will," Captain Jack repeated stepping out of the shack, trace-like. "Right this way, sir."

The Captain began to wobble down the pier. The career fisherman had an odd limp, like Ratso Rizzo in Midnight Cowboy. Myra was asleep on the bench. Jonas doubled back, scooped up his daughter and had to sprint to catch up to Jack.

"She alright?" The Captain asked escorting them to the boat.

"Falls asleep on long drives."

"Count your blessings. My kid has motion sickness. His mother's fault. She coddled him. One day I took him fishing. We stayed out for three days, little bastard ended up getting Thalassophobia, you know, fear of the sea. Now he and his mother don't talk to me. Going on 19 years."

Captain Jack stopped next to the boat, gleaming with pride. It's fiberglass hull still moist from the morning dew. Jonas, however, was not as sentimental. For him, the Nuwave was a means to an end, pure escape. He climbed aboard and disappeared into the cabin with Myra. He reappeared empty handed, palms up and pointed at Jack. The Captain flippantly gave him the keys.

"I'll get your line," Jack said with an accommodating tip of his straw hat.

Jonas settled behind the controls and started her up. The boat's twin diesel inboards roared. Ripples of waves coughed up from under her stern. The Captain untied the boat from the dock and watched his Nuwave maneuver down the narrow peninsula en route to the vast Atlantic. He was both delighted and confused, but had no clue as to why? Jack had just entrusted his $400,000 Sea Ray, his pride and joy, arguably his sole purpose for living, to a complete stranger and he didn't even get a name. Clueless, but happy, the Captain limped back down the pier all smiles.

On the populated streets of Bucharest, Romania, a blind man sat on milk creates in front of the Sofitel Hotel, shaking a can and begging for money. The old man was scruffy, disheveled. Both his eyes were milky and absent of pupils. Liam Dougherty stepped out of the hotel and deposited some coins in the can. The old man smiled a toothless heartfelt smile. Dougherty patted the old man on the shoulder. The old man returned the gesture by mumbling something in Romanian. Perhaps the blind man saw more, with his other heightened senses than he was letting on?

Bucharest was the capital city of Romania where the surrounding Carpathian Mountains served as an aesthetically pleasing backdrop. The Sofitel Hotel was located in the commercial epicenter of an economy on the rebound with all the bells and whistles that the crowds implied. The traffic, the decibels of noise and the mass confusion were leading indicators that tourism was trending upward.

Dougherty crossed the slender cobblestone street to meet with an old colleague at the Café Damovita. When Liam arrived, Father Randall was already at the crowded outdoor eatery, holding a much sought after table and baby-sitting a bottle of wine. Randall was older than Dougherty, but not by much. He was dressed in full priest garb. Liam walked over to his buddy and the men hugged, before sitting.

"I trust the accommodations are adequate, Liam?"

"Yes. Thank you."

"You look fit."

"Stomach is acting up."

Father Randall laughed. "Romanian cuisine is an acquired taste. I took the liberty of ordering us something less harsh, more digestible. Mittitei." Dougherty frowned at Randall before he could translate, "grilled Romanian hamburger. And of course, cock-a-leek."

"Soup?" Dougherty winced.

"It settles the bowels."

"I can't remember my stomach reacting this way during our missionary work."

"You were younger. Your body, more forgiving."

"How long has it been?" Dougherty asked.

"Yankees beat the Braves in six games to win the World Series."

" '96? Good lord. That long? Still say Grissom beat the throw." Dougherty paused. "Don't imagine you catch many games here?"

Father Randall withheld a reply. He forced a smile before looking away. Dougherty continued to probe.

"Was it worth it Anthony, you staying here? Are you happy?"

"Fulfilled. I like to think I made a difference. Saved a soul or two along the way. But then again I wasn't the one with the high aspirations."

"Lately, I find just making it through the day is a noble fight," Dougherty admitted. "And if I can squeeze in a game or two at the stadium every now and again, I'm thrilled."

The waitress brought over the soups. Dougherty was uninspired as his eyes hesitantly dropped down on what appeared to be a piping hot bowl of mud. "Good for the bowels, huh?"

"The trick is not to look at it," Father Randall advised. "So what brings you to Romania my long lost friend?"

Dougherty brought a spoon full of sloop to his lips and cringed during the entire first mouthful. "Anthony, there is a lot I can't tell you. And for that I apologize."

"No need. I understand."

"My diocese has reason to believe that "Terminus is in Cluj.""

Father Randall became noticeably rattled. "Always believed that the final chapter of the bible was a myth. Its existence has never been proven."

"Revelations is inconclusive," Dougherty pointed out. "The older King James version of the bible alludes to a continuance."

"Still, the Archdiocese sent you all the way to Romania on speculation?" Randall raised his glass. "Business must be good." Father Randall finished his wine and nervously reached for Dougherty's cigarettes. "May I?"

"I'm not your cardiologist, Anthony. Help yourself." Dougherty paused. "Who is Alexandru Khrushchev?"

Father Randall took a long drag on the cigarette. His chest expanded out of proportion, challenging his shirt buttons as he filled his lungs up with the sweet intoxication of American tobacco. Savoring the taste, Randall slowly methodically exhaled in short shallow breaths.

"Khrushchev was a great warrior. In 1989, he orchestrated the Romanian Revolution. For some time now, dark tales have surrounded him and his manor. Tales of excess and insatiable perversions, drug abuse and cannibalism. Unsubstantiated, of course. No one from the church wanders from the city. This country is not like when you were here, Liam. There is much lawlessness in the hills."

"Where do I find this Khrushchev Manor?" Dougherty asked unflinching.

Father Randall motioned with the wine bottle as he refilled his glass. "The northern province. Understand this, there is much danger in those mountains. I will take you there in the morning."

"Out of the question. It's too dangerous, you said so yourself."

Father Randall took another drag of the cigarette. "What kind of friend would I be if I permitted you…?"

"Anthony, I did not come here to put you in harms way."

"Your quest, Liam, is grand," Father Randall stated only half believing it. "God will be with us."

A half-mile or so from the new thriving Bucharest, tucked away down a dead end side street of no particular importance, and hidden between two other embarrassing relics, a shoemaker and a candle shop, the local library resided. A decree was handed down by the powers that be at the height of the city's renaissance, all unwelcome reminders of the old order of things that were banished to the outskirts of town to make room for the Starbucks and Chipotle Grills born out of the franchise boom. The tiny, dingy and empty library stood in a forgotten, neglected and in a perpetual state of disrepair. Dougherty was at a back table with a tower of historical reference books in front of him. He was buried in a thick publication entitled, "*Romanian Conflicts*". He thumbed through chapters on the Balkin War and the Romanian invasion of Hungary. He stopped at the section of the Romanian Revolution. He skimmed the text and turned the page. There was a black and white photograph of Alexandru Khrushchev dressed in a full rebel outfit. Below his distinguished picture was Alexandru's affiliation; Commander of the National Salvation Front. Further down the page, Dougherty read the sub text, "*Timisoara Revolt.*" Photos of the then Communist regime of Nicolae Ceausescu, including Mayor Petre Mot. A montage of pictures depicting, rioters looting, violent protests, cars burning in the wake of the repressed in revolt. Haunting photos, a filmed record of the government's atrocities; Nicolea Ceausescu, 70 years old and his wife Elena, standing at the gallows where three children, barely in their teens, were hung. Another picture showed Nicolae and Elena walking hand in hand in the wintry frost, among dozens of naked malnourished Romanians. And lastly, at the bottom of the page, a snap shot of Nicolae slapping a woman across the mouth with his walking stick.

Dougherty lowered the book and rubbed the confusion from his eyes. Alexandru Khrushchev was regarded as a hero in just about every history book Liam was able to get his hands on. He was a liberator and a selfless champion of the repressed. By ridding Romania of Ceausescu, Alexandru saved hundreds of thousands of lives. A complete contradiction to the rumors Father Randall fed Dougherty during lunch. He presented Alexandru in an entirely different light and unflattering light, as an eccentric warmonger holed up in his castle, indulging in bouquets of excess. Dougherty conjured up long tables overflowing with food, wine and sins of the flesh. It was a lust fest, a smorgasbord of naked depravity throwing themselves at an ex-freedom fighter.

If the whispers were true, why the dramatic turn around? It didn't add up. But then again, nothing about the assignment made much sense. The one constant in all the bullshit, there were two sides to every story, and then there was the truth.

Meanwhile, just a stone's throw away, a mere 4800 miles away, the Nuwave sat motionless on the emerald colored waters of Cape May, New Jersey. The glow from the full moon billowed in through the port windows, illuminating the master stateroom where Myra slept peacefully in the twin bed, unbeknownst to Jonas. He sat slouched in a nearby rocker under a dimming desk lamp and continued to read Captain Underpants to his daughter. Jonas finished the chapter and checked on Myra. He closed the book, got up from the chair, and walked out of the room stretching.

Jonas stepped out on to the deck of the boat for some fresh air and to do a little fishing. The lights on shore twinkled sporadically. In the distance, the Cape May lighthouse, the silent sentinel of the sea, blinked routinely signaling to everyone and no one simultaneously. Jonas closed his tired eyes and once again inhaled the invigorating ocean, as it helped replenish his soul. He extended his arms, turning his palms upward. Suddenly, fish began leaping out of the water and onto the deck. Loud slapping interrupted the calm as fluke, blues and mackerel bounced off the inner sides of the boat, creating quite the seafood lovers meal, a meal fit for a king. Dozens of fish flopped around, flaunting their stuff at the mercy of Jonas. After careful consideration, he selected a sizable pair of blues and walked toward the galley as the rejected fish parted at his feet offering him an unobstructed path. Jonas waved his arms a final time, before ducking below. The fish slid up and over the sides of the boat, in a jittery rewind fashion, and belly flopped back into the ocean, leaving a slippery residue in their wake.

The galley was alive with the sound of sizzle as Jonas stood at the stove frying up his catch of the day. He looked up at Myra standing in the doorway, and for the first time in her young life, her complexion was normal. Gone was the unnatural gold skin tone of Crigler-Najjar Syndrome. The child's chronic jaundice was no more.

"Guess I owe you an explanation," Jonas said. "Allow me to introduce myself. I'm your—"

"I know who you are."

Jonas flipped the fish. More Sizzling. "Hungry?"

Suddenly, in his mind's eye, it wasn't Myra standing in the doorway, but Anna. Jonas' eyes welled up with tears. He quickly looked away from his daughter in an unsuccessful attempt to mask his emotion.

"I'm sorry. It's just that you have her eyes," Jonas confessed.

Myra walked over to her father to console him. Her marking peeked out above her pajama top as she reached up to hug him. Jonas hugged back and held on as if he were clinching to dear life itself.

"Don't be sad, please," she said.

"There is much you need to know little one. But first you must get well. Rest will bring you strength. Soon you will be better than new." Jonas pulled away. He looked directly into his daughter's eyes. "But I never wanted to desert you."

"It doesn't matter. I knew you'd come back for me."

Jonas noticed the child's marking. "You must safeguard your mother's messages. It is a delicate balance. We must tip toe among them."

Jonas placed his hand on Myra. His long fingers folded around her tiny shoulders, emitting a series of tingling sensations. The child's body reacted to the throbbing with a universal wiggle as if it were an itch impossible to reach. Suddenly, like chalk to an invisible eraser, Myra's markings began to vanish.

CHAPTER SIX

Outside the Sofitel Hotel, an elderly woman was sweeping the deserted sidewalk in the chill of the morning. An old Mercedes was idling at the curb. Growing impatient, Father Randall spun the rosary beads that hung from the rear view mirror. He checked his watch and nervously looked up and down the street. No sign of Dougherty. Randall began tapping on his steering wheel and involuntarily looked at his watch again. *Where the hell was Liam?* He wondered. Dougherty used to be one of the most punctual people Father Randall knew. But that was a long time ago. Perhaps, he picked up a few inconsiderate habits since they've been apart. Something wasn't right. The priest opened the crowded glove compartment and withdrew a .38 revolver. Randall checked that the gun was fully loaded and tucked it into his pants.

The hotel lobby was bustling with activity. A kid was hawking newspapers next to the revolving doors. A group of French tourists were studying a Romanian map and synchronizing their itineraries. Father Randall walked up to the front desk. Florin, an associate of the hotel, greeted him with a pleasant smile.

"How may I help you, Father?"

"I'm suppose to pick up my friend and he's late. I'm sure he overslept. Can you ring his room, please?"

"Certainly," Florin picked up the phone. "Room number?"

"Uuh, sorry, I don't know."

Florin sidestepped over to the computer. "Last name?"

"Dougherty. Liam Dougherty."

Florin input the name into the computer, spun around and detached an envelope from the message board.

"Mister Dougherty offers his apologies. He left this for you."

Florin handed Randall the envelope. The priest quickly opened it and read the note; "...*sorry old pal. Decided to cab it. Safer for you on the sidelines. Keep the faith! D...*"

Father Randall squashed the note. "Damn!" he hollered. Surprised, by his outburst, guests in the lobby gave Randall more than a passing glance.

Deep within the Carpathian Mountains, a dilapidated cab slowly made its way through the heavily wooded back roads. The sound of the cab straining to change gears, during the upward trek, echoed like little claps of thunder. The cabbie, Henric, an overweight local in a sweaty tee shirt, was behind the wheel. Dougherty was in the back seat, struggling to sightsee through the windows' caked on grime. A ticking sound of debris hitting the car as the woods met the undercarriage was a constant. Henric was heavy on the gas, but even heavier on the brake. The ceaseless jerking motion was beginning to take its toll on Dougherty who nearly lost his breakfast twice—at the foot of the hill and during a two wheel skid that almost sent them tumbling down a 20 foot embankment. The radio was blasting. The reception was terrible and the noise only served to fuel the confusion as Justin Timberlake's "Sexy Back" cut in and out. Henric was a pleasant enough gentleman. His attempt to make Dougherty feel at home by engaging him in a conversation, or Henric's best efforts at conversation, were duly noted by Liam and appreciated. But truth be told, Dougherty would have preferred silence.

"…My brother lives in America. I visit all the time," Henric commented in broken English.

"Whereabouts?"

"New York. You know New York? Big place."

"The biggest."

"Where you come from?" Henric asked.

"New Jersey."

"Oh, Tony Soprano, no?"

Dougherty laughed. "Yeah. I guess so."

Henric cranked up the radio and began to sing. "…Dirty babe—la la la—I'm your slave—" Henric looked at Dougherty in the rear view mirror. "You like?"

"Justin's great."

Henric's eyes dropped back down to the road in the nick of time. He slammed on the brakes. The cab stopped short, everything inside shifted and bounced around including Dougherty.

"What is it? What's wrong?"

Henric pointed to a fallen tree blocking the road. "I know other way." Henric said. "No worry."

The cabbie threw the car into reverse and that god awful grinding noise reared its ugly head. It sounded as if the transmission was about to drop out of the cab on the spot. Henric floored it, the cab spun around kicking up an enormous dust cloud as it plowed into the thick brush. Scraping, rippling and tearing as Henric mowed down every shrub, weed and small tree in his path.

Henric continued singing on key but completely out of sync with the song. "…I bringing sexy back…them others don't know how to act…go 'head be gone with it…"

The cab slowed down as it approached a rickety old bridge, suspended over the Dambovita River, 70 feet below.

"No worry. I cross this bridge on many trips," Henric assured Dougherty. Liam wasn't buying it. Skeptical, he crept up to the edge of his seat and remained vigilant, eyes glued to the teetering crossing. The cab crawled onto the bridge. Its wheelbase was too wide for the rotted wooden span as a third of the tires hung off the side. Liam heard creaking, the sound of wood snapping, above and beyond Justin Timberlake's "Sexy Back." Tense, the slouching cabbie sat upright with almost perfect posture, hands planted firmly on the steering wheel. Henric wiped the perspiration from his forehead and turned off the radio with the same hand. There was no time for music. The business at hand required total concentration. There would be plenty occasion for song when and if they made it to the other side. Henric's eyes widened, darting right to left, left to right, ever cognizant of the bridge's width. Dougherty stuck his head out the window and assisted in the navigation.

"Easy, easy. You're OK on this side."

Liam spoke too soon. Mid way across the fragile span, he heard a whipping noise. Dougherty looked up and saw one of the bridge's support ropes unraveling and ultimately drop into the river. The bridge lisped to the left, creating unsustainable pressure on the deteriorated planks, causing the cab's back tire to crash through the floorboard. In an attempt to drive the tire out of the crater, Henric accelerated. But the tire only spun in place, sending up splinters of petrified wood and rusted decay, while the bridge swung wildly.

"Don't move!!!" Dougherty yelled.

Henric closed his eyes and silently prayed. Both men held on hoping the bridge would stabilize. On the other side of the crossing, the Reapers were hiding in the thick brush, watching and waiting as the cab dangled half on, half off the bridge.

"When exactly was the last time you came this way?" Dougherty asked.

Henric took a long moment. "7 years ago, on foot…"

The bridge continued to sway. Dougherty and Henric remained frozen in their respective spots, afraid to create the next vibration, a vibration that could surely kill them.

"What do we do now?" Henric asked.

"Cut our losses and jump."

"This car feeds my family. I will push it across. Not much further." Henric opened the passenger side door.

"Hold it!" Dougherty yelled, before Henric could put a leg out. "Since we're already in place, its easier if I push and you give it the gas. Easy! Don't floor it."

"OK. Whatever you say."

"Wait till I get out." Dougherty opened the car door, rolling his eyes. "Hope you can swim"

From the underbrush, droopy little eyes continued to stare. The Reapers grunted to each other, as they grew restless. More rustling, more scurrying as they repositioned themselves exposing their lower extremities of misshapen legs with thickened skin, riddled with boils of various shapes and sizes.

Bare feet, some webbed, others fused together into one filthy big toe as they limped into place.

Dougherty got out of the cab and strategically placed himself behind the car, both hands on the fender directly above the troubled tire. He peeked down through the missing floorboard at the 70-foot plunge into the raging white-capped river.

"We go on three. Ready? One—two—three!!!"

The cab's engine roared as Henric accelerated. A series of loud pops rang out. Dougherty assumed it was the car's exhaust, until the windows shattered and he realized it wasn't backfire, it was, in fact, gunshots. Dougherty froze in place. In the distance, he saw the Reapers hobbling onto the bridge from both sides, still too far off to make out any of their hideous characteristics. More shots. Dougherty ducked. He watched helplessly as Henric got hit. The cabbie jerked and twitched as bullets ripped through his flesh, He instinctively put up his hands for protection, but the shots were coming from all directions. He was shot in the hand. His palm exploded from the blast, blowing off his thumb and index finger in the bargain. His blood splattered on the slivers of remaining window as a trail of bullets tore across the trunk of the cab. Tires exploded. Dougherty felt a hot stinging sensation in his side, which he shrugged off, until a perfectly symmetrical blood stain spread across his shirt. Liam was shot. He folded over, staggering backward, and fell over the side of the bridge. The severed suspension rope was barely within his reach, and with the angry river rushing up behind him; Dougherty grabbed the rope, catching it in mid flight. His free fall was momentarily stymied as he swung violently from the convulsing bridge. The cab sunk deeper into the broken floorboards, snapping more wood under the uneven weight. As Dougherty attempted to pull himself up, he realized that he was in the cross hairs of a Reaper's rifle. A quick glance revealed to Dougherty that the grotesque Reaper had a face riddled with nodules, small rounded lumps from ear to ear and forehead to chin. In between the labyrinth of knotted dermis, was a reservoir of oozing puss. The Reaper's nose was crooked and twisted in the shape of a cockeyed "U". Its eyes were disproportionately spaced. One bloodshot, the other absent all together, just a dark empty crusty hole, in a shockingly repugnant face. It was crunch time for Liam, time for a quick decision. If he held on to the rope, it was certain death at the business end of a Soviet SKS carbine. Or Dougherty could dive into the furious river and battle a powerful undertow that would be a challenge for the best of swimmers. Liam decided to take his chances with the watery grave and released the rope just as the gunshot was fired, figuring with any luck, his neck would snap on the way down, killing him instantly, painlessly. Dougherty hit the water feet first. He remained totally submerged under the thunderous roars of the mighty rapids. Liam's hand popped out and fumbled around for something to latch onto. Dougherty found a rock and pulled his head out of the water long enough to witness the cab crashing through the bridge and plummet toward him at an incredible speed. Dougherty submerged himself under the surging waters as the cab slammed into the rock belly up. The impact sent the rock's pronounced peak through the bottom of the cab and out the sunroof. The blood splattered windshield imploded from the force, skimming the rapids as a gyrating projectile. The carriage of the cab remained impaled on the rock, while its doors were simply washed away. Dougherty battled the impossible current, and clawed his way back to Henric for some 11th hour heroics. The cabbie was motionless, however. Dougherty attempted to free him from the seat but an uncooperative jagged metal piece from the car's interior had speared Henric through the upper leg. Out of the corner of his eye, Dougherty could see Reapers gathering on the bridge and taking a marksmen stance.

More shots were fired. Bullets whizzed by Liam as he tugged on an unresponsive Henric. The leg remained stubborn, its flesh stretched as the metal tore through more of the snagged leg until bone was visible. Dougherty firmed up his grip, a grip slippery from being water logged and continued to yank and tag until a sizeable chunk of Henric's thigh ripped off in a red gush, freeing him. The piece of leg sunk like a stone in the now bloody waters. Dougherty held Henric, supporting his head above the river and allowed the turbulent waters to carry them off.

Dougherty fell victim to the in between. He was neither dead or among the living. Liam was in an altered state of indifference. This stagnant status opened his subconscious in the most profound ways. Sure there was the proverbial tunnel drenched with radiant gleam, but the promise of what awaited him on the other side, wasn't what you'd expect nor was it a happy ending with a saintly narrative or an angelic choir stroking their finely tuned harps underscoring a reconciliation sanctioned by the divinities. Benito, stood at the entrance. He was in his 60's with stern features, the unflinching idiosyncrasies of a fascist dictator.

"Buon Giorno," Benito said with a thick Italian accent.

"Maybe you can help me. I'm lost."

"I doubt it. We are all right where we belong."

"I'm Liam, Liam…"

"Dougherty. I know who you are Father. Been expecting you."

"Who are you?" Liam asked looking around. "What is this place?"

"My friends call me "il duce". Since we are not comrades, I'm Benito to you."

"Am I in Hell?"

Benito laughed. "Don't be so dramatic. What is it with you pompous Americans and your theatrics? You are where you are. Do you accept your sentencing?"

"I've done nothing wrong," Dougherty maintained forcefully.

"Then appeal. You don't necessarily have to stay here." Benito pointed his shaky, arthritis's ridden finger at the tunnel. "Prove your sinlessness! Walk the walk!"

Apprehensively, Dougherty looked beyond Benito. There was an undeniable allure, a menacing charm, much like the attraction of a high school bad boy to the virgin sophomore. It was an awakening of sorts and Dougherty felt compelled to take the plunge, deflower the perils before him, but he dared not move.

"What's on the other side? Heaven?" Liam asked.

"Again with the drama. The light is more of a discharge from your spiritual debt, an emotional bankruptcy."

"What's in the tunnel?"

"You tell me. They're your demons. Arrivederci."

"Wait." Dougherty shouted, but it was too late, Benito was gone. Liam hesitantly stepped into the passageway just as the tunnel went dark. The dazzling glow from the other side lit his path, but created forebodingly long shadows. It was soundless, except for faint cries of infants. The tunnels nothingness frightened Dougherty. It was isolation so profound it took on an almost physical application as if Liam could reach out and touch the solitude, the ex priest's sequestration. Dougherty wanted nothing more than to get to the other side and so as his pace quickened, the babies' crying intensified. The passageway narrowed. The walls were closing in. Dougherty began to run as fast his legs would carry him, but it was no use, he was running in place. The tunnel's exit remained elusive. It's light seemed further away as if Dougherty was running backward on a very cruel treadmill. The walls became rubbery and faces appeared, ghostly and distorted. The unrecognizable mugs of demons past and present, pressed against the impressionable walls stretching them all out of proportion. Skeleton-like arms sprouted from both sides of the passageway and reached for Dougherty. He was able to dodge a few, but ultimately Liam was caught and pulled toward the animated walls and its pulsating images. Dougherty resisted with such conviction, the soles of his shoes tore apart and curled up as he tried to maintain traction and his distance. But in the end, in death as in life, evil overcame him. Dougherty had succumbed to the forces that be and allowed himself to be yanked into the wall.

Once again, Dougherty returned to St. Vincent's Hospital, moments before the fateful blast, where Arthur Shields stood in the maternity ward behind the visitor's glass, gawking at the newborns and patting his bomb belt. Shields brought the detonator to his lips and kissed the weapon of mass destruction. The infants were crying at the top of their tiny lungs, as if they instinctively knew.

"This is for you Father Dougherty. Its all for you…" Arthur obeyed unconditionally the ranting of his deranged mind and ignited the explosives. There was a quick flash. The carnage came in silent waves of ruin as the immeasurable tragic loss of life ensued. Or did it? As the smoke cleared, out of the ashes of annihilation, from the foggy haze of debris and fresh from the fight, Dougherty rose up out of nowhere. He stood straight as an arrow, steadfast in his resolve, perfectly poised in front of the bassinets, which were miraculously unscathed by the blast. Liam's arms were fully extended outwardly at his sides, in an ancient messiah fashion. Instantly, the sound of infants crying resumed, shattering the dead silence. It was music to Dougherty's ears, but there was still much more to be done. Liam turned his palms down and the infants immediately levitated up out of the basinets in spirit-like fashion and floated

toward him. Delighted, Dougherty welcomed them with the
warmest of smiles. Then, unexpectedly, disappointingly, Liam
reverted back to the despondency of real life…

Dougherty had washed up on a riverbank, lying motionless
on his back with his legs still in the water. He coughed up a
mouthful of river and opened his eyes to Lucian Puravet
rubbing his chest. Lucian was 10 years old with chubby kid
cheeks and shoulder length hair.

"You alright mister?" the kid asked earnestly, looking down
at Liam with great concern.

Dougherty withheld a reply, turning on his side, shielding
his eyes from the annoying sun. Sophie Puravet, Lucian's
mother, ran over to offer her assistance. She was in her early
30's and the epitome of understated beauty, tall and plain with
the most amazing olive colored eyes.

"Oh, my God," Sophie gasped, kneeling down next to
Liam. "Is he breathing?"

As she gave Dougherty the once over, she noticed the blood
soaked shirt and immediately concluded that the stranger had
been shot. Sophie's knee jerk reaction was to leave him on the
riverbank and permit nature to take its course. It was certainly
an option and who would blame her? She had the safety of a
young boy to think about. But the God fearing, Christian do-

gooder in her emerged to cast aside any dark intentions, leaving a man to die would not be Christ-like behavior. Surely, the Lord would watch over them all. It was, like every thing else, a test of faith.

Dougherty spit up more water as he began coughing uncontrollably.

"Lucian, quickly, lets get him to the house," she said, struggling to help Dougherty up on his feet.

The Puravet residence was a simple wooden A-frame house nestled somewhere in the Carpathian Mountains. It was a nice size piece of property with an adjunct barn and clusters of sheep roaming about freely. Inside the guest room, the furnishings were shabby hand me downs, a twin bed, mismatched night tables, a dresser with an undersized mirror. It looked like the direct result of a swap meet gone bad, but it served its purpose. Dougherty was in bed, bare chested and zoning in and out of consciousness, an occasional groan slipped out of him as Sophie did her thing. She was seated next to him with a needle and thread, sewing up his gunshot wound while Lucian stood on the opposite side, holding the stranger still. It appeared to be a clean shot, the bullet entered and exited without nicking any bone or vital arteries. But Sophie wasn't a physician, making it impossible to speculate. She had seen these kinds of wounds rapidly turn ugly. Inflection was the villain, the variable, which traveled seemingly at the speed of light. Sophie was mindful of this and she would have to remain vigilant and step up her treatment. A bottle of Slavic brand Vodka sat on the crowded night table and served as both a mild anesthetic and a sterilizer. A rusty basin filled with bloody wash cloths, additional needles and a pair of scissor also occupied the night table. Sophie, a seamstress by profession, administered the final stitch, pulling the needle through Dougherty's stubborn skin, as she tied the thread and snipped off any excess.

"Is he going to be alright, Mama?"

"There's nothing left to do but pray," Sophie whispered, admiring her signature zigzag needlework and collected the spent cotton balls. As she turned to walk out, Dougherty grabbed her arm.

"Thank you," Liam said hoarse, his pale face contorting from pain.

"Rest," she replied.

Dougherty's hand slipped back down at his side. Sophie and Lucian walked out, closing the door behind them.

In the kitchen, Emile Puravet, was sitting at the table, thumbing through Dougherty's wallet. Emile was older than his wife, by at least a decade. He was heavy set with thinning hair flopping from side to side susceptible to drafts and the likes. Sophie walked in as her son raced past her.

"Going down to the lake to see if anyone else washed up." Lucian said breathlessly, passing through the kitchen like a pre-adolescent tornado.

"Mind your chores, young man."

"I will," Lucian fired off an empty promise before bolting out the door. Sophie walked over to the stove and began preparing food.

"How is he?" Emile asked.

"The bullet grazed him. He's banged up a bit, but he was lucky."

"Should we call Doctor Stolojan?"

"Do we have the money?"

"No. But he does." Emile pulled a hand full of the bills out of Dougherty's wallet.

"Put it back, Emile!"

"He's a priest, you know. From America."

"Who told you that?"

Emile took out Dougherty's Clergy identification and flashed it at his wife.

"He's a long way from home. What's he doing here, Sophie?"

"Missionary work?" She blurted out the first thing that came to her mind, knowing from experience that seldom does the obvious hold true.

"The Church has long given up on us," Emile smirked as the mocking began in a manner he knew drove his wife crazy. After 15 years of marriage he knew all the right buttons to get a charge out of Sophie. "…Blessed are the villagers of Cluj for they are sure to perish—slowly."

"Stop it! Don't blaspheme!"

"You haven't answered my question Sophie…what is he doing here?"

"You're just gonna have to wait and ask him."

"Think it's a matter for the law."

"Show me a policeman with the slightest regard for the law and I'll gladly make the call. Until then, put the money back, Emile!"

Reluctantly, Emile stuffed the money back in the wallet. Sophie swiped the wallet out of his hands and shoved it in her apron.

"It'll stay with me for safe keeping."

"Oh, I get it," Emile laughed. "Tall, dark and handsome. He's a man of God, Sophie. Don't you blaspheme!"

"You're disgusting!"

Back on the rickety old bridge, Father Randall and his sidekick, Toma Savu, were combing the crime scene looking for clues. Toma was short and stocky, dressed in a soiled tank top and equally dirty shorts. His excessively hairy shoulders were desperately in need of some manscaping and Toma appeared to have insect phobia. He was constantly swatting away bugs, some tangible, most imaginary as he involuntarily scratched his psoriasis-riddled arms.

Randall carefully examined the broken floorboards, covered with spent rifle casings and followed an alternating trail of blood to the edge of the bridge.

"Careful, Father!" Toma warned in broken English. "Careful!"

Father Randall noticed the severed support ropes, visually following them down to the smashed cab and the raging Dambovita River. Toma hesitantly ventured closer to the edge, mindful of his footing and checked out the considerable drop.

"No way. No way your friend could have survived that fall. No way in hell!" Toma offered before realizing that he was talking to a man of the cloth. "Sorry, Father…"

Father Randall and Toma scoured the immediate brush below the bridge as well. Flummoxed, Randall walked to the river's edge, studying the empty remains of the impaled cab, then he turned his attention down stream at the roaring rapids.

"Even if the lucky bastard survived the fall," Toma said scratching his head, "there's no way he wasn't crushed by these rapids. Impossible. It would take a Goddamn miracle…" Toma caught himself, but again it was too late as Randall fired off an irritated look. "Pardon my foul mouth, Father. What I mean to say is no way your friend is alive. No way!"

"Where does this river lead?"

"This far north? Could fork off in a dozen different directions. If he did survive, which he did not, he could be anywhere. Guess you're just going to have to wait until he contacts you."

"Search them all!!!" Randall insisted.

"But I don't have the manpower…"

"Make no mistake about it, Dougherty and I go back a long way," Father Randall angrily clarified. "He deserves a decent burial. And I'm going to see to it that he gets one. Understood?"

CHAPTER SEVEN

At the Puravet residence, Lucian was spending yet another night in the guest room with Dougherty, it was becoming one of his favorite pastimes. The attention-starved lad sat next to the bed, whimsically humming various songs, which floated, in and out of his head like musical poltergeists. Lucian was patiently watching, waiting, hoping that the stranger would soon wake so he'd have someone new to talk with and hopefully befriend.

And to Lucian's delight, that evening, Dougherty slowly opened a crusty eye. Liam immediately grimaced, his body screamed with pain. A sudden bolt of inflammation scampered from his gunshot wound, around to his tailbone, back to the wound again, coming full circle.

"Momma…," Lucian hollered with excitement.

Sophie walked in and smiled. "I see the fever broke. That's good. How are we feeling?"

"Been better." Dougherty assessed with a mouthful of raspy dryness. Liam struggled to sit up. He draped his heavy legs over the side of the bed as he attempted to shrug off another wave of agony. This time not just from the wound, every muscle and joint weighted in with a formal complaint of acute stiffness as if his entire anatomy had been dipped into a generically altered, liquefied vat of Viagra. In Dougherty mind, he believed that rigor mortis had already set in, in anticipation of his imminent demise.

"Easy. Mind your stitches," Sophie warned.

"How is Henric?"

"I'm sorry, who?" She asked.

"The cabbie, Henric. He was with me on the bridge. He needs my help. Quick… there is no time."

"That was three days ago," Sophie exclaimed in an attempt to curtail his desperation. "Your friend is probably no more. Or there is very little left of him."

"I have to notify the police. Our attackers, these hideous things came out of no where…" Dougherty reached for his cell phone, but only its empty case remained clipped to his belt.

"The high fever. You were hallucinating," she offered up a plausible explanation, but Dougherty wasn't buying any of it.

"Do you have a telephone I can use?"

"Not since the storm." Sophie nodded, taking a breath. "I'm Sophie Puravet."

"Liam. Liam Dougherty."

"Nice to meet you Mr. Dougherty. This is my son, Lucian."

"How are you doing, kid?"

Lucian's eyes widened. "You got shot."

Concerned, Dougherty looked at Sophie for confirmation.

"Grazed. You were lucky," she said. "Hungry?"

The Puravet's kitchen was buzzing for the first time in years as the aroma of a well-cooked meal permeated the air, pleasing the senses. Everyone was huddled around the busy table, handing off food in a counter clockwise rotation. Sophie and Lucian were blatantly fawning over their new houseguest. Liam represented an infusion of mystery, the allure of the unknown, a welcomed modern sigh of freshness into the dregs of the family's mundane dinner conversation. However, Emile was not impressed. Leery of anyone from the west, thanks in part to local bigotry, and the extreme condition in which Liam was found, presented too many variables for Emile to rest easy and enjoy his wife's Tocanita stew. As the self-proclaimed head of the household, he wasn't about to permit himself to be hoodwinked. Caution and an abundance of it, was the word of the day.

"So what business do you have in Cluj, Father?" Emile asked.

"It's Liam. I'm no longer a priest. At least not in my heart anyway."

"Turned your back on the calling?" Emile pushed.

"Emile," his wife rolled her eyes.

"What? I'm making conversation, that's all..."

"Let's just say the calling became so faint, I could no longer hear it," Dougherty explained.

"Pity," Emile said. "And you are in Cluj because…?"

"I did some missionary work in Romania a while back. I'm here visiting old friends."

"Old friends that didn't warn you about these mountains are not really friends." Emile smirked loading a spoonful of stew into his mouth.

"They tried. I wouldn't listen."

"More Saramura, Father—sorry, Mr. Dougherty." Sophie offered picking up the plate.

"It's Liam. And yes, please. The carp is excellent. Thank you."

"It too salty as usual," Emile chimed in.

"I would like to report the attack to the authorities." Dougherty said as Sophie shovels more food on his dish.

"The hills are full of bandits," Emile answered as his facial muscles began to twitch.

"It didn't seem like they were interested in money."

"How many were there?"

"A band. A gang. All misshapen. Horribly deformed…"

Sophie and Emile looked at each other. There was a secret in their eyes.

"I got a good look at one of them," Dougherty continued. "Could probably give the police a description."

"Want my advice?" Emile asked rhetorically as his speech began to slur. "Forget the police. Trust no one…"

Emile's slurring worsened. He stared at Dougherty blankly as if he was looking through his houseguest. "No one is as they appear. No one."

Liam wondered if he was the only one hip to Emile's rapid deterioration? And if it was as obvious to Sophie and Lucian, why were they being so nonchalant about it? Only one reason leaped out at him. Emile's transformation was a common occurrence and his loved ones had become desensitized to it.

"What my husband is trying to say is the police, sometimes do not take kindly to strangers."

"Well, I'd still like to get to a telephone."

"If you feel up to it, tomorrow I will bring you into town and you can make your calls."

Lucian perked up as his face brightened. "Can I come?"

"If you complete your chores and finish your dinner plate, why not?" Sophie said.

Lucian's fork began to speed up. Segregation was too time consuming, so he mixed his vegetables, potatoes and fish into a colorful glob and swallowed it whole. Emile's glass dropped out of his hand and shattered on the wooden floor. Everyone's attention turned to the head of the household, who was now expressionless, his complexion, a paler shade of white. His body trembled as the violent seizure took hold. The steady drool barely noticeable out of the corner of his mouth was widening as food particles soon accompanied the waterfall of saliva. Sophie sprung up, rushing to the aid of her husband while Lucian continued to eat unruffled. Dougherty's fears were confirmed. Emile was sick, very sick and his behavior was a matter of course that his family had, over time, become immune to. Fearful of her husband choking, Sophie pried open Emile's clinched teeth, reached into his mouth and removed any remaining chunks of unchewed Saramura. She quickly walked behind Emile and wheeled him from the table. He was wheel chair bound; a home made concoction with a wooden body, a wheel from Lucian's old tricycle, the other off a wheel barrel.

"Will you excuse us?" Sophie asked without conviction.

"Is your husband alright?"

"No, Mr. Dougherty. He is not."

Emile continued to convulse as his wife wheeled him down the hallway and into a back room.

The dawning of a new day brought an unwelcome overcast to the mountains and an even less desirable steady mist in the air. An all-encompassing gray sky was beset by storm clouds that raced with great earnest above the Puravet residence, preceded by rumbles of thunder in the distance.

Behind the house, Dougherty was loading breadbaskets of grain and fruit into the wagon. Sophie walked out of the barn with Tatiana, the nine year old Philly that was left to the Puravets when their cousin from Bulgaria died last fall.   The horse was looking worn, not much spring left in her hoofs, but she was still a ravishing beauty. Tatiana possessed a silky brown coat that appeared as if it had been waxed and buffed by a janitorial team. She glistened even in the gloomiest of days.

"Be careful of your side," Sophie said concerned as she walked over with the horse. "I'll load the rest."

Sophie fastened Tatiana to the wagon and packed the remaining baskets. Lucian charged out of the house like a crazed young boy on a mission.

"Momma, you promised," he yelled sobbing.

"Luc, please stay with your father. He needs you."

"But you promised," the boy insisted, teary eyed.

"You'll come to the marketplace next time. Please Lucian. I'll bring you back a surprise"

"What?"

"Then it wouldn't be a surprise."

Disappointed, he began kicking at the dirt. "Ok."

"Can I have a kiss?" Sophie asked politely.

Lucian took a long moment, but with an impending "surprise" waiting for him on the other end as inducement, he gave his mother a peak on the cheek. Granted, it was a lifeless smooch and rather mechanical, but it would suffice. At least she wasn't dealing with an inconsolable crying tirade or one of Lucian's notorious temper tantrums that always left Sophie with a heavy heart and turned a pleasant enough trek to town into a long day's journey from hell. Sophie climbed up on the wagon and helped Dougherty aboard.

"We won't be long." She waved as Luican stomped back to the house, kicking everything in his path. Sophie grabbed the reigns and the wagon pulled away as Tatiana embarked on a steady trot through the picturesque countryside.

"Good kid you got yourself, Mrs. Puravet."

"The best. He's got to get more fun in his life."

"How long has your husband had ALS?"

"Almost two years," Sophie replied with some hesitation, surprised by Dougherty's accurate diagnosis. "The doctors are not very hopeful."

"It must be very hard on you and Lucian."

"I am alone, even when Emile is with me," she said with overwhelming sadness. "It is as if I live my life in the dark. I wish I knew how long, so I can prepare."

"Three to five years is the life expectancy for Lou Gehrig's Disease."

"Who?"

"He was a baseball player who brought ALS to the attention of the nation," Dougherty explained.

"So not too much more." Sophie looked off as the dire implications crept in.

"There have been cases where patients with the disease have lasted longer. But those are the less fortunate ones."

"Lucian and Emile are close," Sophie said.

"When my father died, I wasn't much older than Lucian. He was a brawny, tough Irish bastard. Worked as a longshoreman, you know, on the docks with ships. Had hands like sledgehammers. Cancer brought him to his knees quick enough."

"I'm sorry," Sophie said lowering her sympathetic eyes.

"What I'm getting at is, it's probably not a good idea to have the kid around. The final stages of ALS are very painful."

"I understand Mr. Dougherty. But Emile needs us. Anyhow, that's tomorrow's sorrow. Today we must be happy" Sophie looked up as the sun played an indecisive game of peek-a-boo behind dissipating clouds. "The weather is clearing. Perhaps with a little faith, it will be a beautiful day."

"Big sky. Something you don't see in Jersey."

The wagon unexpectedly hit a bump. Everything shifted as baskets toppled and Dougherty fell off the wagon. It was an awkward, unsightly spill, head first, legs wrapping around his folded torso pretzel-like. It was the kind of embarrassment you'd expect to see on America's Home Video or You Tube.

"Oh my God," Sophie gasped tugging on the reigns as Tatiana eventually came to complete stop. "Are you alright?"

Dougherty's rebound wasn't exactly stellar. He got up slowly and brushed himself off more flustered than anything else.

"I'll live."

"Mind your stitches." She pulled him back onto the wagon. Dougherty winced as he sat. "How is your side?"

"It's not my side that I'm worried about." He said rubbing his ass. Sophie tried her darnest not to be disrespectful, but she failed miserably and laughed in Dougherty's face.

"Sure. Make fun of the city boy. Why not?" Liam blushed.

Sophie signaled Tatiana with a light yank on the reins and the trip resumed, but a slower more prudent pace and with a serious knocking sound coming from the wagon.

"Feel that?" Sophie asked.

"I can't feel a thing. My whole body is numb."

This time she didn't even try to hold anything in, Sophie just flat right laughed as the wagon continued its journey wobbling and slanting on the passenger side.

The road into the marketplace was bottlenecked. Wagons and cars were parked along side each other, horizontally, vertically, perpendicular, and haphazardly in no particular order. Villages were coming and going with shopping carts filled to the brim with goods. Festive Romanian music played continuously, pushing the single speaker's capabilities to the point of distortion with its persistent bass. Roasters and chicken chased themselves in a stylized impromptu version of Ring-o-levio, wings flapping, feathers flying. Sophie and Dougherty parked the wagon wherever they could and headed inside, buckling the demonstrative crowd.

The marketplace was a giant flea market of sorts with wall-to-wall locals bartering and haggling at the top of their lungs with merchants over ridiculous prices and biased trade practices. Livestock roamed freely down the aisles, tripping up everyone in their temperamental path. Animal dung covered with saw dust littered the floor like tiny indiscriminate land mines. Horse flies executing a precision aerial assault, dive-bombing onto the fresh excrement to plant their flag, then re-ascending to calm bragging rights. Some returned, others did not, turning their mission Kamikaze. Dougherty snaked his way through the chaos looking for a phone.

"Telephone? Where's the phone?" Dougherty stopped a worker. The under age teenager with a nametag, pointed in the opposite direction. Liam battled his way against the crush of foot traffic, arm protecting his side mindful of his stitches, until he came to a pay phone directly in front of the restrooms. He fumbled around his pockets for change, picked up the receiver and as Dougherty fed the telephone, he noticed a gruesome face in the crowd staring at him. Distracted, Liam dropped some money, he briefly took his eyes off the face in the crowd, looked down and watched the coin roll into a mound of crap, before toppling tails up. Dougherty didn't dare. There was no way in hell he was going to retrieve it, the coin was a goner. When Liam looked back up, the disfigured face had vanished into the masses.

"Hello? Hello Anthony? It's Liam…," he announced into the phone and loudly due to the bad connection. "Man, am I glad to hear your voice. It's a long story. Suffice to say partner, I will never doubt you again…"

After his telephone call, Dougherty stepped outside to the lesser of the disorganization. With his pounding head still reeling from the commotion, Liam lit a soothing Marlboro and took a long relaxing drag. He held the smoke in his expending lungs; it was a bittersweet reunion as Dougherty savored the cool menthol taste. It had been days since his last butt and it was a relief that his jittery withdrawals would soon be coming to an end.

Liam panned the parking area for the hideous man that followed him to the phones. Sure there were some locals that were hard on the eyes, sporting Quasimodo-like humps and bad teeth, but no one that could be classified as truly horrifying. Maybe it was Dougherty's fatigued mind playing tricks on him. After all, for God's sakes, he had been shot. And how many priests back in Trenton can lay claim to that? Or perhaps it was a copulation of elements, inefficient lighting, the herd of people and the incessant stench of shit whirling around his nostrils and challenging the senses. Dougherty did see Sophie emerge from the marketplace with an arm full of supplies. He immediately crushed the tip of his cigarette with his thumb and index fingers and slipped the balance of the butt into his shirt pocket for safekeeping as he rushed over to offer his assistance.

"Did you get through?" Sophie asked, loading the bags into the wagon.

"Yes. Father Randall is picking me up in the morning."

"Still think it is premature. Rest another day. What's your rush?"

"Are we done here?" Dougherty queried, propping the last of the supplies against the back of the seat.

"No Mittitei. Lucian will be disappointed, but yes we are finished."

Dougherty helped Sophie up into the wagon. She instinctively grabbed the reins. A dramatic pause ensued as Liam looked at her somewhat disenchanted.

"You promised." He said, refreshing her memory.

"Fine." Sophie sighed, rolling her eyes and sliding over to the passenger side. A smile came to Dougherty slowly as she handed him the reins. Excited, Liam hopped up into the wagon in a single graceful motion.

"Hell, I'm a city boy. I may never get another chance like this again." Dougherty noted, slapping down on the reins.

Tatiana was far less enthusiastic. Maybe it was the animal's keen senses picking up on the naiveté oozing from Dougherty's pores or simply his limp wrist, the non-committal manner in which he clutched the reins, imparted his inexperience. Either way, the horse began her monotonous trot back home.

The evening air had an old fashion chill up its sleeve. Its stillness unabashedly interrupted by a gentle breeze, brushing the trees that hung over the Privet house like giant pom-poms and creating a swishing sound against a backdrop of cricket chatter. Still, the cloudless umbrella sky was both cinematic and humbling. It was breathtaking, peaceful, deceivingly so. Dougherty stood on the back porch with drink in hand admiring the starry countryside. *If there truly is a God, he does nice work*. He thought.

The screen door opened and slammed with a rusty creek as Sophie walked out and softly crept up behind Liam, brandishing a bottle of wine. Her perfume, stronger than usual, infiltrated the immediate area and quickly spread to the livestock grazing in the field.

"I want to thank you, Mrs. Puravet, for all your kindness."

"What do I have to do to get you to call me Sophie?" He asked not expecting a reply. "More wine?"

"I'm fine. Thank you."

An excessively long silence followed needlessly, in part because the lonely homemaker was waiting for the "right" moment. The notation that a "right" moment existed was falsehood, a myth, and the etiquette world's equivalent to Santa or the Tooth Fairy. Assuming there was a "right" moment, it has certainly proved capricious, elusive at best, a time that may never come. So for the second time in her unfulfilled life, Sophie threw caution to the wind and spoke her mind.

"Why are you in Cluj, Liam Dougherty? And please don't lie to me."

"I was on my way to Khrushchev Manor."

"Why? People die there in unspeakable ways."

"Church business."

"Thought you said that you are no longer---."

"I'm not. It's complicated."

"How does a man of God turn his back on his faith?" Sophie asked, exacting the truth. Oddly, the normally tight-lipped Dougherty felt compelled to tell her. He wanted to confide in someone, why not the person that saved his life? His attraction to this woman, this stranger, this nobody, kept him off balance. He suddenly longed to confess, but there wasn't a confessional in sight. Liam hungered to leave the ugliness of his transgressions in the forgiving hands of his healer, but the clergy had long deserted him. Everyone had abandoned Dougherty; accept this woman, this stranger, and this nobody. And once Liam began his divulgence, he couldn't stop. As it turned out the cleansing of one's soul is as addictive as oxycontin.

"There was this guy under my care." Dougherty surrendered to his diarrhea of the mouth. "Now Arthur had some emotional issues. Yes, he was quirky and could be morose at times, but I never pegged him as dangerous. In my report, he was categorized as harmless. Imagine that? One day, one god forsaken day, Arty walks into the maternity ward of a local hospital and blows himself up. Took a bunch of infants with him. Their tiny arms and legs strewed all over the place. Mr. Harmless proved quite insane and I never saw it coming. So in a few weeks I embark on a new career at the college. What is it they say? Those who can't do, teach."

"Why did he kill like that?" she asked innocently with a look of disbelief.

"Arthur found life unfair. It was his chief complaint. I guess he wanted to spare the newborns the horrors of a future." Dougherty raised his glass and with every ounce of sarcasm he could muster. "Here's to the Dougherty Report, it isn't worth the paper it's written on." Liam took another mouthful of vino.

"But it wasn't your fault. How could you have known the evil that resides within?"

"You're sweet." Dougherty smiled. "I never told anyone that story before. Anyhow, I'm a sinner, Sophie. Nothing more. Nothing less."

"Repent, Liam. God doesn't forgive because of who you are. He forgives because of who he is."

Dougherty finished his drink. Although appreciative of the kind words, it was obvious that he wasn't buying it.

"Its late. If I don't see you in the morning, thanks again for everything. God bless you and your family." Dougherty kissed Sophie's cheek. She closed her wanton eyes and leaned into him. Liam broke away and walked into the house.

The dead of night fell hard upon the Puravet household. The pitch black isolation had returned like a long lost friend, surrounded on all sides by nothing, and the continued prospects of nothing, took its toll. In the guest room, Dougherty stood in front of the dresser mirror and removed his shirt. He examined the purplish bruises, while running his finger over the gunshot wound and its bumpy stitching. It seemed to be healing nicely, and although infection could not yet be ruled out, it seemed unlikely from the looks of things. The room was lit only by the flickering of candles and the phantom menaces they produced. A beaten man in crisis, the bitter cynic believing again in what was once shrouded in doubt. The anti-hero raging a furious battle against temptation while being trapped in an imperfect body in which its flesh burned with unconscionable desire. And then there was the damsel in distress, the lady in white, a lonely woman ensnared by her quiet hours of desperation. Suddenly, yet quite expectedly, this heroine appeared to Dougherty through the reflection in the mirror. Liam turned; Sophie was standing in the doorway. Two strangers faced each other and squared off void of words and innuendo; their eyes said it all as they bared their soul without shame. Sophie soundlessly closed the bedroom door and like a sultry vision, she tip toed toward Dougherty. Her footsteps were light as a breeze; the face of an angel masked Sophie's hedonistic intentions. She gradually unbuttoned her nightshirt and slid it off one shoulder at a time until the covering slithered down her curvy body, hitting the floor as quiescently as a feather. Sophie stood before Liam, an unabashed temptress as her chest heaved recklessly in perfect synch with her untamed heart. Dougherty could resist no longer as he filled himself with her sweet intoxication. It was a bloodless Coup D'etat, the direct result Liam had toppled, and he had been happily overthrown. In Dougherty's mind's eye, Arthur Shields leaned in from out of the shadows and whispered in Liam's ear.

"Bellissimo…,"Arthur said, without taking his eyes off Sophie. Shields leaned back and once again disappeared into the obscurity of Liam's subconscious.

"Emile?" Dougherty asked.

"My husband wants me to be happy?" Sophie replied in a velvety voice, her bedroom eyes narrowing. Gingerly, she tested the murky waters by groping Dougherty. Her trembling hands skated across his body with long sweeping strokes over every ripple of his bare chest. Liam closed his eyes. He was over sensitive to her touch. Sophie's fingertips were scolding, like tiny irons against his percolating flesh, as she pried and explored.

Adjunct to the guest room, the Puravet's boudoir was dark and soundless. Barely visible was Emile silhouette, in his wheel chair with his face pressed against the wall. He was watching with envy while sobbing uncontrollably. Emile was witnessing Sophie's carnal antics through a crack in the wall and overwhelmed by both revulsion and gratitude. He was revolted that the situation had graduated to such a state. Shouldering most of the blame for his chronic uselessness. It was more a disease of the mind, than his physically deteriorating condition. Once a lethal dose of guilt crept into his consciousness, his impotence perpetuated, and seeped into his engine room where it killed his erection quicker than potassium chloride. Yet Emile was grateful to Dougherty that Sophie was not being deprived the intimacy she so richly craved. Regardless of how justifiable his wife's actions were, it was something a husband could never get use to. So engulfed by the affairs of the heart, Emile was oblivious to the rustling and the chatter outside the house as a dozen or so Reapers invaded the property. The freakish assassins fanned out and surrounded the house.

Back in the guest room, Dougherty stood behind Sophie at the foot of the bed. Liam was holding her pressing body against his as they swayed in place, eyes closed, savoring the moment. He placed his hand on her shoulder and began to bend Sophie over. Penetration was a fluttering heartbeat away, as were broken vows and a betrayal of biblical proportions. Just how many of the lord's commandments was Dougherty planning on breaking on his reckless plight to perdition? Enter upstage right, Liam's Christian guilt as the pangs of culpability shot through him; Liam became quite paralyzed with trepidation. The cabbie came to mind, as did the commandment, *"Thou shall not kill"* And although his death was still unconfirmed, Henric was undeniably MIA and presumed dead by those in the know. Granted, Dougherty didn't directly pull the trigger, he was responsible for getting the cabbie on the bridge and putting him in harms way. As for, *"thou shall not covet your neighbor's wife,"* Dougherty would have to plead no contest and throw himself on the mercy of St. Pete. Or would he? Liam abandoned his own heart by stepping away from his burning desire and Sophie. She ran back into his embrace. Dougherty pushed her away and kept her at a distance, mindful of his wavering will power.

"I'm sorry, I can not!" Liam said unconvincingly. "Forgive me, but I can not."

In the Puravet's bedroom, tears were streaming from Emile's face. Suddenly, he heard a noise too suspicious to ignore. He pushed himself away from the wall and turned his undivided attention to the disturbance.

Meanwhile, back in the guest room, a defeated Sophie bowed her head and gently wept. Much was said by the couple's awkward silence. But when the neglected housewife finally looked back up at Dougherty there was acceptance in her teary eyes. Sophie submitted to her predicament, conceded to the loneliness, embracing it, in fact, like a long lost friend, her only constant. She graciously bowed to Liam's attack of conscious, his decision, in the nick of time, not to betray his faith. Despite Dougherty's Herculean denials, he was still very much a priest in his heart. If nothing else, that became abundantly clear to Sophie and it was that look of understanding that exonerated Liam of all wrong doings.

Before she was able to verbalize those emotions, there was a crashing sound from somewhere in the house. Dougherty rushed to the door, opened it a crack and peeked out in the darkness. There was another crash and the shattering of glass.

"Lucian…," Sophie gasped, charging for the door.

Dougherty kept her in the room and silenced her by placing a finger over his lips. When Sophie found her composure, Dougherty opened the door wider.

In the Puravet bedroom, two Reapers crept up behind Emile. Emile was in his wheelchair, still with his face toward the wall. Soundlessly, one of the Reapers removed a machete with a sliding noise of cold steel meeting cold steel. He raised the instrument of death and aimed it at Emile's head. Emile spun around and emptied both barrels of his shotgun into them. The first blast lifted one Reaper off the ground and sent him sailing across the room. The reaper slammed into the wall and slid to the floor a bloody mess as plaster and wall debris showered down on him. Muzzle flare from the second shot provided the room's only light, like a flash photo as it captured the other Reaper's head exploding like a watermelon. It was truly a Kodak moment as brains and pieces of skull splattered about like a pop art exhibition showcasing deranged Andy Warhol paintings. As darkness returned to the room, there was the sound of the Reaper's headless remains toppling over with a wet thump.

Another Reaper crashed through the window of the guest room and charged at Dougherty. Sophie screamed and bolted out of the room. The creature tackled Dougherty, climbed on his chest and began strangling him. Liam struggled to break free but his assailant was a powerful little bastard and for a fleeing moment, Dougherty thought he would lose consciousness and for his sins his life would end in that room. Dying, however, was not an option; he had Sophie and the kid to think about, so he battled back. Liam slapped and punched, by shifting his body right to left, left to right it repositioned the Reaper, his grip loosened allowing some air into Dougherty's starved lungs, buying him a little more time. Arms flapping, the priest moved around some debris and spotted a piece of broken window frame on the floor. Dougherty reached for it, stretching his arm almost to the point of dislocating, but it was no use, the frame was simply beyond his fingertips and would remain out of his reach no matter how hard he pulled and clawed and attempted to wiggle toward it. As fate would have it, Liam got assistance from an unlikely ally. Yet another Reaper, brandishing a handgun, barreled into the room to wreak havoc but instead inadvertently kicked the window frame closer. Dougherty wasted no time; he picked up the frame and hit the Reaper repeatedly, driving the frame's protruding rusty nail into his face and neck. A red gush jetted out from one of the puncture wounds as the Reaper sprung up, releasing Dougherty. The Reaper grabbed his squirting neck and staggered around the room in a frantic haze as if he were performing some cockamamie ritual dance. The shorter Reaper fired at Dougherty. The shot missed him by mere inches. It would have been a kill shot, dead center in the priest's solarplex had he not immediately rolled away. Instead the bullet harmlessly enlarged in the wooden floorboard as Dougherty whacked the creature in his Achilles heel, nail first. The Reaper shrieked, it was a high-pitched howl direct from the bowels of hell, as he wildly sprayed the room with bullets until his gun was empty. The other Reaper was hit with friendly fire, once in the eye and again in the chest, and collapsed on the bed. As the shorter creature tried, in vein, to remove the window frame that was nailed to his ankle, Dougherty darted out of the bedroom and into the hallway where Emile was reloading his shotgun. The head of the household fired at a fleeing Reaper, but missed, blowing a king size hole in his refrigerator. Sparks flew out and cascaded onto the kitchen floor like hundreds of illuminated pellets, joining the rolling apples and swirling pieces of singed milk carton. Emile fired again. The blast hit the couch as the Reaper jumped out the window leaving an explosion of feathers in his wake. The buckshot also took out the television and both lamps simultaneously. The house became unbearably smoky. Dougherty's eyes were tearing as he gagged on his own dryness. Emile wheeled toward the shattered window, reloading for what he hoped would be the final time. Spent shells hit the floor with a hallow thud interrupting a sudden eerie calm.

Dougherty followed the crying into Lucian's bedroom, where Sophie and her son were cowered in a corner. The kid was petrified; crying persistently as his mother covered her baby's eyes from the dead Reaper sprawled out in his closet, a half a foot away. The creature had a hole in his chest the size of a basketball. There was simply a cavity where his vital organs were once housed; some remnants of the Reaper remained, like his exposed rib cage swimming in a mound of indescribable goo. Much of his innards had oozed out of him, so much so that the kid's area rug was floating in a reservoir of bloody discharge. There were more gunshots. Sophie and Lucian flinched.

"Is he alright?" Dougherty asked.

Sophie nodded, kissing her son's forehead. The bedroom door busted open wide, Emile wheeled in.

"Son-of-a-bitch got away!"

"They'll be more. They won't stop. They know I'm here," Dougherty said. "Is there anywhere you and your family can stay tonight?"

"Yes. Mr. Bianca down the road," Emile replied. "And you, Father?"

Under the cover of night, Sophie quickly ushered Dougherty out the back of the house. Emile sat on the porch with his shotgun in his lap, keeping a watchful eye out for Reapers or anything else that might go bump in the night. He was fully prepared to shoot first and ask questions later, a house full of dead creatures was testament to his mindset. Being head of the household had its privileges.   Sophie disappeared into the barn and when she reappeared, she was holding Tatiana.

"I will return her to you," Dougherty vowed taking the reins from Sophie.

"No. You must get out, Liam. As far away from Cluj as she will take you and you must never look back!"

Dougherty caressed Sophie's tear stained cheek. He would remember her tenderness forever, as well as her infectious smile eternally imprinted on his heart. Sophie kissed his hand, savoring the moment, knowing full well that it would be the last time she would ever see the priest.

"I've got to make one last stop," Dougherty announced over her objections as he mounted the horse. "Are you guys going to be alright?"

"Yes." Sophie forced a smile.

"I'm so sorry for putting your family through this. I promise you, by morning, it will all be over."

Dougherty dug his heels into Tatiana and the horse galloped off into the night. With a heavy heart, Sophie watched as Dougherty was swallowed up by the darkness.

CHAPTER EIGHT

With the wind at his back, Dougherty rode the nine-year-old Philly through the dense brush, to a clearing of sorts that brought them to a narrow path along the Dambovita River. The roar of the rapids coupled with the horse's thunderous gallop bounced off the darkness and echoed through the deserted countryside. Tatiana trotted pass a familiar site, the scene of the crime, where the stripped frame of Henric's cab still sat in the river and the dilapidated suspension bridge was now a violent vibration away from total collapse. Before long the ominous mansion on the hill came into view. Dougherty had business at the estate. Personal business to settle with its proprietor, whoever, what ever he was. So with the senseless disappearance of Henric the cabbie, and the safety of the Puravets, Liam kicked it up a notch as he continued north to Khrushchev Manor.

As Dougherty approached the main gate of the Manor, he hopped off his horse and fastened Tatiana to a tree a few yards away from the entrance. The mansion on the hill wasn't exactly what he was expecting. But Liam learned early on in the seminary, never to judge a gothic manor by it's curb appeal. Its run-down, almost abandoned appearance added a certain foreboding charm to its stereotypical creepy demeanor. It was easy to understand how the hyperboles of dark tales and strange events originated. But then again, Dougherty left behind a shitload of misshapen assassins, so he wasn't about to take any chances.

Khrushchev Manor was steeped in Romanian history and probably built around the turn of the 17th century. The Manor consisted of three floors or wards and occupied 7 acres of land with Tudor timber-framed buildings scattered about the grounds. The estate was a transition between a stone faced old fortress and a more atheistically pleasing mansion suitable for the likes of a land baron or a knight; true suburbanites that wished to reside in the land of gallantry. The manor's daunting gatehouse and walled bailey must have been both majestic and menacing in its day but was now an ivy-mantled ruin, another example of vanished glory. Its massive wrought iron gates boldly displayed the initials *AK* on top with tarnished gold lettering. Dougherty snuck up to the guardhouse and looked inside at the Reaper asleep, webbed feet up on the desk, in front of a snowy black and white television, Dougherty noticed that the gate was ajar and slipped in unannounced. Once on the grounds, Dougherty saw that the manor was dark, except for a light in a second floor window. He used it as his beacon, his true north. Dougherty walked toward the light combating the high weeds and other annoyances of a neglected landscape. Dogs began to bark, big hounds judging by the growls. Dougherty's pace quickened as hugged the shadows and crept to the back of the mansion, where he tried a pair of doors. Both were locked. He found a basement window, but it too was locked. Dougherty sent his elbow crashing through a pane of glass, and then he reached in and unlocked the point of entry.

Liam climbed through the broken window down into the dark, dingy basement. The place stunk beyond the obvious musty, mildew odor, this was much more pungent. Suddenly memories of high school flooded through Dougherty, his thoughts returned to gym class—sweat socks. Yes, that was it. The basement reeked of wet sweat socks and used athletic supporters. This must be the place where old sweat socks and jock straps are laid to rest, the last stop where all laundry service terminated. Liam followed the wall around and through another gate into what could have conceivably been a wine cellar at some point. Dougherty heard a chorus of squeaking. And with every step he took, the squeaking intensified. Liam looked down at the colony of rats scurrying away, racing over his shoes in a rodent version of tag. If it weren't so disgusting, it would have been comical to watch the little fellows' rapid, exaggerated pace, as they knocked into themselves and trampled over each other in clumsy Keystone Cops-like fashion. It was like watching an old silent movie. Dougherty heard footsteps, irregular footsteps coming from outside. Suddenly, a beam of light from the broken window, followed by a Reaper peeking in as his flashlight panned the basement. Instantly, Dougherty ducked behind a marble counter and breathlessly watched the light float past him. The Reaper mumbled something to himself, obviously the creature wasn't satisfied, and so he took Liam's identical path, descending into the basement through the shattered window. With his flashlight in one hand, and a gun in the other, the Reaper began his methodical search. From behind the counter, Dougherty studied the Reaper's crooked feet as he wobbled forward. The squeaking ramped up as more rats ran for cover. Dougherty carefully, soundlessly, snaked around the counter and sprung up behind the Reaper, surprising him. The creature spun around as Dougherty smashed him in the kisser with a right and then a left punch followed by an uppercut just for good measure. The Reaper fell backward, out cold even before he hit the rancid floor. The gun and the flashlight hit the ground as well, but unfortunately the gun took a nasty bounce away from Dougherty and was lost in the darkness. The light began to roll into a corner, but Liam retrieved it in mid pivot and was finally able to shed some light on his situation, quickly discovering that he was in a crypt of some kind and that the marble counter was, in actuality, a marble sarcophagus. Dougherty examined the coffin for any inscriptions, but there was nothing. His initial attempts to open the tomb were unsuccessful; the weighty lid would not budge. Realizing that it was going to take some elbow grease, Dougherty put down the light and braced himself against the back wall. He firmly planted both hands under the lip of the lid and pushed with every ounce of strength he had, until the soles of his shoes began to peel up from the sheer force. Even with giving it all he had, the lid only partially slid open. Dougherty picked up the flashlight and aimed it inside the sarcophagus at the skeletal remains dressed in a general's uniform. Doors flew open and the florescent lights came on overhead as the Reapers flooded the crypt with their guns drawn. They shouted Romanian gibberish, first at Dougherty, then among themselves. Liam held his hands in plain sight, but defiantly hollered back at them.

"Take me to Alexandru Khrushchev!!! Dougherty's demands seemed to spark more arguing between the Reapers. "Did you hear me?" Take me to Khrushchev!!!"

A Reaper stepped out of the group, pointed a gun in Liam's face and cocked it. Dougherty closed his eyes anticipating the fatal shot at any time. For Liam, it would confirm the age-old question that had pledged him of late *"is there truly a God?"* Just a simple twitch on the hairpin trigger, doesn't even have to be voluntary, and the secrets of the universe will be open to him. The other Reapers were egging the assassin on; he was about to shoot the priest…

"Wait…!" Toma shouted as he pushed through the crush of Reapers and walked up to Dougherty with morbid curiosity.

"I want to see Alexandru Khrushchev!!!" Dougherty barked his demands at a new face.

Toma gave Liam a pitiful once over and smirked, motioning to the sarcophagus.

"You already have." Toma said, and then turned to the Reapers. "Bring him to the lord."

A wave of protests erupted so demonstratively, he found it necessary to assert his authority with a holler that rattled every bone in the crypt.

"At once!!! The lord is waiting…"

A heavily armed entourage of creatures took Dougherty to the study for some quality time with the man in charge, the Lord of the Reapers. Liam was impressed almost immediately; normally a person would have to visit the Vatican to confront this level of gaudiness. The study was gargantuan, suitable for a king more than adequate for a mere lord, spewing absolute excess at every turn, "*no wonder Europe lost the war*" floated in and out of Dougherty's head. It was grand-scale with 14-foot ceilings; every amenity detailed in hand carved oak. Scary looking oil paintings hung across the long wall, portraits of the lord's demonic counterparts. Shelves filled to capacity with rare books collected from around the world, took up the rest of the wall space. Priceless volumes of religious works banned by various cultures, their authors were visionaries, but labeled Heretics by the ruling class. They were guilty only of being vastly ahead of their time. It was an collection reading that would rival the most comprehensive libraries of Romania, quite possibly Western Europe.

The Lord of the Reapers kept his back to the action, choosing instead, to stare out of the oversized bay window at the rolling hills of Cluj while fondling an animal of sorts in his arms. One of his loyal servants shoved Dougherty closer to his highness.

"Kneel in the presence of the Lord!" The Reaper hollered whacking Dougherty in the back of the leg with the butt of his rifle. Liam dropped to one knee, without taking his eyes off the Lord. There was something hauntingly familiar about him.

"For God's sake Liam, get up. I'm really as humble as apple pie."

"Anthony?"

The lord turned to Dougherty. It was Father Randall, dressed in full priest garb and petting, with long strokes, a gray brush tail possum.

"Don't mind telling you, you've been a real pain in the ass. Anyone else would have high tailed it back to Jersey. But I'm afraid this move was predictable."

"Father Randall, you got some '*splaining* to do." Liam said doing his best Ricky Ricardo impression.

"I might as well complete the picture." Randall shrugged. "We'll call it a last request."

"Where's Alexandru Khrushchev?"

"Dead by my sword. But I'm getting ahead of myself…"

And so Father Randall began to 'splain' in vivid detail about the revolution and the pounding the National Salvation Front was taking. Ceausescu and his communist regime had brought the rebels to their knees with constant shelling. Deep within the Carpathian Mountains, Alexandru Khrushchev and the rest of the resistance were retreating. The government had once again squashed another attempt at a coup. Alexandru dodged explosions as well as the bodies of fallen comrades that were strewed across the blood soaked hills. Clouds of smoke floated around the battlefield like phantoms in the nightmarish fog of war, so it was no wonder Alexandru didn't immediately see Grigore on the ground, flapping around in pain. Alexandru doubled back and helped his comrade to his feet, and then they made an ill-fated run for the top of the knoll. It sounded like a good idea at the time. A mortar shell cut their trek short, landing a few feet away from Grigore. The impact knocked Alexandru down while it sent Grigore gyrating in the thick air like a Frisbee sailing through the heavy humidity of a mid August beach day at the Jersey shore. His flight ended abruptly when, as a matter of happenstance, a tree popped up unannounced and intercepted the freedom fighter. Grigore smashed up against the tree with such force, the snap, crackle and pop of his bones shattering, could be heard from yards away. Alexandru, face covered in soot, crawled over to him and although it was still attached, Grigore's head was twisted completely around 180 degrees. His chin now rested between his broad shoulder blades as the young freedom fighter died with his stunned blue eyes wide with a surprised look etched on his face. As Alexandru reached over to close his comrade's lifeless eyes, he noticed an object protruding out from the crater the explosion produced. Alexandru wiggled closer and saw that it was some kind of cylinder. He dug it out with his hands and examined it more thoroughly. Against his better judgment, although truth be told, Alexandru was not expecting to survive the battle, he began to open it. Suddenly, Grigore gasped as he opened his eyes and stared unflinchingly up at the heaven.

"STOP!!! And heed my warning young warrior…" The dead freedom fighter issued with a fusion of different voices.

Startled, Alexandru turned to a motionless Grigore. He rubbed his face in his hands; his body shuddered in an attempt to shake off the mental atrophy, attributing the hallucination to the haze of war.

"Grigore?"

"Your friend is gone. Lost forever to the cause."

"Who are you?" Alexandru asked, still only half believing his own eyes.

"That is not important. You are at the crossroads of your fate. You hold in your hands the balance of good and evil. Unlock the mystery and you assume complete responsibility."

"Responsibility?"

"Keep it out of the hands of evil until the dark pope's thousand year reign is up and it is retrieved by the very hand of God. In return for its protection, you will be granted the wisdom of a thousand leaders, the strength of a thousand warriors. And truly I say unto you this day, you will triumph over tyranny and oppression for the next thousand years."

"Al right, I guess…" Alexandru faltered.

"Choose wisely." The deceased warrior pressed firmly, unconvinced and sensing Alexandru's ambiguity. "Make no mistake, should the scriptures fall into the wrong hands, all will be lost. There can be no redemption. Do you accept your destiny?"

There were more blasts, blood, guts and debris showered down on Alexandru.   He withheld a reply, momentarily distracted by the cluster of explosions. Alexandru panned the horrific battlefield and witnessed the continued slaughter of his follow countrymen. The screams, the pleas, the prayers were suddenly amplified, challenging Alexandru's sanity. A nod of his head, a simple twist of a lid, and the suffering would end, it would all go away.   Alexandru had the power, the absolute power, absolutely. Perhaps too much power for one man to wield.   Alexandru couldn't take it any longer, the odds were fifty/fifty that the offer was bogus anyhow, born of stress and fatigue. He had to mute the relentless voices in his head, so he opened the cylinder, of course he did.   Griore gasped a final time and his eyes slowly closed, content that Alexandru Khrushchev took charge of Terminus.

As promised Alexandru was granted the wisdom of a thousand leaders and the strength of a thousand warriors and he took the fight directly to the steps of the central committee building with a massive anti-government rally on Timisoara Square. Nicolae Caeusescu, the ruthless leader of Romania was on the balcony addressing the people in a last ditched attempt to calm the unrest. His wife, Elena was at his side and also screaming at the masses. There were explosions in the streets, plumes of smoke billowing in sections of the square. The sound of automatic gunfire rang out. Tear gas was fired at the crowd, the canisters spun wildly in the streets spewing noxious fumes as chaos ensued.

"Wake up Romanians. We are the people. Have no fear, Ceausescu will fall." Alexandru's amplified voice of encouragement came through a bullhorn.

The murderous regime sounded their sirens, but could not drown out the cheers. The revolution unfolded and what a glorious afternoon it was. A resurrection of sorts as if the tombs had opened and out poured, in a euphoric gushes, squinting from the blinding light of day, the suppressed, the stymied, the confused, the militants and the ashamed. All speaking with one resounding voice and a single collective gasp that resonated like a clash of thunder over the brutal dictatorship. The rally turned into a violent protest as the rebel backed crowd stormed the building with their heads held high, chests out, holding hands in a perpetual chain of unity that spanned across the repressed country with a juggernaut of expression, put an end to tyranny.

In the new order of things there was no room for bitterness or anger, hatred or contempt. The former things were no more, cast out like the narrow-minded. The intolerant were powerless; finally their hatred was not able to contain the outbreak.

Warmongers and dictators wallowed in their own debauchery as the peaceful took back their liberties. Of course, there were still some I's to be dotted and a few T's to cross and the courtyard of the central committee building seemed like the ideal place to start.

Nicolae and Elena Ceausescu stood up against the wall with their trembling hands tied behind their backs. The courtyard was filled to the rafters with bloodthirsty on-lookers. A confidant Alexandru stepped out from behind the executioners and walked up to the couple.

"You have been found guilt of genocide and crimes against the state."

"I've killed thousands. And I will kill thousands more. I do not apologize for taking a single life." Nicolae remained defiant to the bitter end as he spit at the crowd. "Burn in hell!" Someone yelled out before the entire courtyard began chanting,"*we are the people*" Alexandru stepped back. The executioners raised their AK-47 assault rifles. With a wave of Alexandru's hand, they fired into the couple, ending the dictator's 21year reign of terror. The rebels had successfully overthrown the government. The crowd roared with liberated exuberance. They charged at Alexandru, lifting him up on their shoulder and carried him off an instant hero.

Back at the study, Randall wrapped things up and he finished a glass of old wine.

"And that my friend, is how the west was won."

"Thanks for the history lesson, but that doesn't explain…"

"I know," Father Randall beat Dougherty to the punch. "What's a dazzling urbanite like myself doing in a gothic setting like this? Mind-boggling isn't it? Truth is, it wasn't my doing, not initially. Funny how cultures view things differently?"

In Father Randall's mind's eye, he flashed back to simpler, more lascivious time. He remembered, with sentiment and fondness, standing at the alter of innocence, surrounded by dozens of bare chested young boys. Randall was sipping wine and offering sacred sacrament.

"Back home my indiscretions were frowned upon." Randall recalled. "I was labeled a degenerate and spit on. Here, my indulgence is viewed as a harmless vice and I'm worshipped…"

"They threw you out, I hope."

"I was simply shipped off to a place where I would cause minimal embarrassment. So for my sins, they sent me back to Romania. Those first few weeks here were brutal."

"Poor baby."

"I must confess that I thought about taking my own life on several occasions. Spent most of my time roaming the streets in a drunken stupor. One night, I wandered into the wrong part of town. The Reapers found me..."

"Reapers?"

"The off shoot of a leper colony that once resided in the mountains. Anyhow, they robbed me, beat me and left me for dead in a drainage basin under the overpass. I remember the incessant sounds of water cascading and woke up in a sewer on the outskirts of town, under this very Manor. I was soaking wet..."

Once again Father Randall brought Dougherty back in time, if only in their minds, to the very sewer on that fateful night when Randall was knighted a servant in Satan's service. Rats scattered. The long shadow of a fleeing rodent projected on the sewer wall, and then suddenly transformed into the shadow of an approaching woman. LILITH swaggered toward Father Randall with the cool class of a Hollywood starlet. She was stunningly beautiful, with tight shiny ringlets of long jet-black hair that bounced invitingly with every strut and wiggle of her scantily clothed quintessential hourglass figure. She had black lifeless eyes, tan complexion and the promise of eternal ecstasy on her pouty fiery red lips. Lilith was much more than Randall could handle and enough woman for the priest to give up young boys forever. Captivated by her loveliness, Father Randall never noticed Lilith's lengthy scaly tail oscillate from side to side before coiling up and retracting into her back. Randall, like most men, didn't want to see a demon approaching, as he was in lust.

"You there, I seem to have lost my way. Can you direct me back to…"

"We've been expecting you, priest." She replied in a soft, sexy voice. "I ask, what fruits have your loyalty to the church brought you? In the eyes of your God, you are a blight and an outcast. To us, however, you are the right kind of sinner."

"Get behind me Satan!!!"

"You flatter me, priest." Lilith battered her eyes coyly. "I am not the dark pope."

"Be gone daughter of darkness!!!" Randall waved his hand, but to no avail.

"Don't be naïve, he has fathered us both. Besides, you don't have the conviction to send anyone packing."

"What are you?"

"I am Lilith."

"Lilith?"

"Perhaps you might have heard the suggestion of me? Before Adam and Eve, it was Adam and me."

"I thought you were merely a myth."

"Funny how the undesirable are omitted from history. Surely, you can relate, father"

"If I remember the story correctly, you turned your back on your husband and the Garden of Eden."

"That's one way of looking at it." Lilith smirked. "I choose to see it as my right as an equal. We were created together, yet I was expected to be subservient, the good wife. The June Cleaver of the Old Testament. I certainly could not tolerate such an injustice. My husband was lucky I merely left him. For his endless whining, Adam was finally given his puppeteer, but it cost him his rib. Pathetic runt."

"Story has it, for your ingratitude, you were made a demon, queen of the succubus."

"I'd rather be a queen in hell, than a submissive dish rag in paradise." Lilith took a dramatic moment. "I offer you the same."

"What do you want from me?"

"Simply to take back what is rightfully ours."

"What do you mean? Stop talking in circles, demon!"

"It's been in front of you all the while." Lilith pointed to the wall. She broke off her index finger with a snap that echoed throughout the sewer as a new digit immediately regenerated. She dropped her detached finger on the floor and it discharged into a dozen crowbars. Lilith raised her arms and summoned an army of Reapers. They filed in, picked up the crowbars and began hammering away at the wall with mighty swings. Before long, a radiant cone of light emanated from the newly created hole. The Reapers parted and the cylinder was revealed. Alexandru Khrushchev had quite foolishly buried the sacred scriptures in plain sight under the Manor. Father Randall was hypnotized by the cylinder's twinkling incandescence. He walked closer, basking in the warm throes of its effervescence; Randall reached into the wall and pulled out the Holy Scriptures.

Alexandru Khrushchev knew he screwed up and like a true Romanian nobleman, he accepted the consequences of his complacency with dignity. He was taken outside the manor, thrown to his knees as a pair of Reapers held him in place. Alexandru proudly bowed his head as Lord Randall drew his sword. It wasn't a stretch to think that Khrushchev spent his final heartbeats praying for a swift and painless decapitation. But there was an excellent possibility that his highness died with Grigore's whispery warning on his mind, "...*should the scriptures fall into the wrong hands, all will be lost...*"

Father Randall swung the mighty instrument of death at the neck of Khrushchev. His severed head rolled unevenly along the wide edge of the blade. Alexandru's terrified olive colored eyes revolved in its travels, upside down, right side up, until eventually flipping back into their sockets never to be seen again. The rest of him, a wet mess, toppled forward, exposing the newly vacated space between his shoulders where his head use to be just moments before. Out of a cavity of pink and redden rawness, a single stream of blood squirted with the irregularity of a premature ejaculation, and began to spread in his foreground. All was indeed lost…

The tall tales wound down, Father Randall finished bringing Dougherty up to speed and they returned to study.

"So Terminus is here?" Liam asked with skepticism.

"The scriptures are in my charge. And in my possession they will remain. We are forever."

"What happens now?"

"Now you die!" Randall exclaimed without the slightest hesitation, motioning to Toma. "Take him into the woods and hang him."

"Afterwards, can we eat him?" A Reaper asked out of turn.

"Curb your tongue! Liam is a friend," frowned Father Randall as he turned to Dougherty. "Gotta love the Reapers. Grant you, they are not the Spartans, but they are mine."

The Reapers surround Dougherty, pushing and pulling at him. Liam resisted initially.

"Tell me Anthony, how do you see all this ending?"

"I don't." Randall said uncommonly relaxed under the extreme circumstances as the Reapers carried Dougherty out.

Outside Khrushchev Manor, the main gates opened and horses thundered out. Toma and three armed Reapers on horseback encircled Dougherty and his horse en route to the woods. Liam's hands were tied behind his back with such conviction, wiggling out of the knots were next to impossible. He did notice that Tatiana was gone and wondered if her vanishing was at the hands of the Reapers or did the horse simply get loose and was safely half way home by now? As the posse rode through the thick brush a single shot rang out. Toma, who had been on the pace horse, was hit. He tumbled backward off the horse and spiraled down a ditch, moaning with every bump. There were several more gunshots and although no one was hit, the noise scared the be Jesus out of the horses, rearing up on their hind legs and neighing at the darkness. Dougherty did not posses a keen sense of survival by any stretch of the imagination, another skill never taught at Saint Mary's Seminary. But Liam appreciated disorder when it was so blatantly staring him in the face, so he took his cue, seizing the opportunity, Dougherty jumped off the horse. With his hands still hopelessly bound behind him, Liam absorbed the brunt of the fall with his bursitis riddled shoulder and somersaulted down a ravine with the grace of a three-legged deer who just took a barrel full of buckshot in the buttocks. More gunshots rang out in the night, from everywhere, from nowhere. Another Reaper was shot. Dougherty kept his head low and wiggled up against a tree for cover. It was doubtful his captors would ever regain control of the situation. There were only two Reapers left and they definitely had their hands full staying alive. Dougherty heard rustling in the darkness, someone was crawling up behind him. Startled, Liam quickly turned and was pleasantly surprised to see Sophie smiling brightly. He was about to erupt with elation. But before he could get a word out, Sophie silenced him with a long, passionate kiss, and then quickly untied him. More shots. Then the manic gallop of the remaining Reapers riding off.

"All clear. They're gone." A voice clamored in the pitch darkness.

Dougherty and Sophie sprang up and brushed each other off. He was favoring his right shoulder.

"Did you remember to mind your stitches?" Sophie asked helping Dougherty back up the ravine to a waiting horse and wagon. Mr. Bianca and Aron walked out from behind the trees. Mr. Bianca was a strapping farmer in his mid 50's, dressed in overalls and a sweaty tee shirt. His super extended belly told Dougherty that he more than likely was on an all-liquid diet, expressly from the Ursus Breweries, Romania's "*king of beers*". The farmer also sported an Indian Jones like fedora. Under the crooked hat, Bianca had a lazy eye that gave him trouble with depth perception, especially at night. Aron was a very intense young man in his early 20's and well over six feet tall. Dougherty could tell that the kid was wound too tight by Aron's one-dimensional expression of continual constipation.

"Quickly!" Mr. Bianca advised.

"Liam, this is Dragos Bianca."

Dougherty and Dragos shook hands. "My son, Aron"

Aron climbed onto the wagon and kept a close eye out for the Reapers, breaking his concentration just long enough to nod in Liam's direction.

"Thank you, both." Liam offered, undeniably heartfelt.

"Come, there is little time." Mr. Bianca said, preparing the wagon.

"They are good men, Liam. They will take you into Bulgaria. From there, you go home!!!"

"Sophie, I—I—" Dougherty was hard pressed for words, possibly the first time ever. Eventually, the right discourse would have come, but Mr. Bianca cut their farewell short.

"Please, we must go now!" He barked. "Soon, it will be daylight."

"You must go!" Sophie mimicked, betraying her heart.

The couple looked into each other's eyes and kissed a final time.

"Thank you again, Mrs. Puravet," Dougherty waved as he lifted himself into the wagon. He lay on his side, squeezing between breadbaskets of goods. Mr. Bianca covered Dougherty with a quilt, and then camouflaged the quilt with blankets. Mr. Bianca hopped onto the wagon, slapped down hard on the reigns and the wagon pulled away. Sophie watched teary eyed as Dougherty faded into the distance. She mounted Tatiana and trotted off in the opposite direction.

Meanwhile, back in the states, more specifically, the Trenton Archdiocese, Monsignor Hayden sat in his dimly lit office, pouring himself a tall stiff drink and staring out the window at the city at play. He was the watchman on duty 24/7 and rest assured nothing unsavory was going to happen on his tour. *Yeah, right!* Hayden thought no longer buying into the cliché and reassessing his relevance with every numbing mouthful of Scotch. That may have been true once, but that was back in the day. When faith wavered less and the distinction between the spiritual world and the secular were more defined, no one dared cross the line. Emotionally drained, he had every right to feel sorry for himself, not only shouldering the weight of Trenton, but there were times Monsignor Hayden felt like he was responsible for the preservation of Christianity. Agent Biggers appeared in the doorway. Hayden tensed up in anticipation of good news, any news about Myra's whereabouts.

"False alarm" The fed said. "It wasn't the child."

The fleeting glimmer of hope slid off the monsignor's anemic complexion. Biggers walked into the office carrying a manila envelope. The Monsignor politely pointed to a chair across from his desk.

"Thanks. But I've been sitting all night." Biggers watched Hayden as he topped off his glass. "A night cap to help you sleep, Monsignor?"

"There isn't enough alcohol in all of South Jersey to help me sleep tonight." Hayden pointed the bottle at the Fed.

"No. Thank you." He nodded. "It's not all bad. We stepped things up. Looks like we're going to get some media help. They'll need some recent photographs."

There was no reply from the monsignor. He remained placid. Hayden downed another belt of booze, than turned his attention and his look of hopeless abandonment toward the window and the animated view of a twinkling downtown Trenton.

"I read the Dougherty report." Agent Biggers said placing the envelope on the desk.

"Riveting, is it not?"

"It's pretty out there."

"Out there?" The Monsignor laughed. "We are in the business of "out there".

"What I mean, is…"

"I'll tell you what's "out there", Hayden interrupted. "Somewhere, "out there" is a sick orphan child. I'll tell you what's also "out there", beyond your "all point bulletins" and nationwide manhunt, Liam Dougherty on church business, missing. They're "out there". Where? God only knows. I'm responsible for both of them. And I don't know if either one is dead or alive. Now that's "out there", wouldn't you agree?"

"You mustn't give up hope, Monsignor."

"Faith is in the heart of the zealot, Agent Biggers." Monsignor Hayden said before returning to quiet. Biggers respected the long silence; it gave them both a chance to recharge. He would start the conversation back up when he felt it was right and not a moment sooner. Biggers relied on his gut instincts on matters such as these, instincts that were correct about 88 percent of the time.

"What do you think we are dealing with here, sir?" The Fed reverted back to his training in the art of interrogations. And although Hayden was certainly not under suspicion, Biggers wanted to keep him talking because you never know what diarrhea of the mouth would reveal. The monsignor laughed.

His merriment was so intense; it teetered on mocking the federal agent. The extent of the laughter was awkward and immediately out of context. Realizing he may have over reacted, Hayden quickly toned it down.

"You'll have to excuse me, Agent Biggers. I'm tired and I hurt and I'm tipsy, or at least I hope to be after another swallow." Hayden proudly held up his glass. "I've had just about enough disappointment for one day. So if there's nothing else, please close the door on the way out, will you?"

"Of course. Sorry to have bothered you, Monsignor. I'll be in touch." Agent Biggers walked out of the office and like a god fearing Christian, obeyed the Monsignor and closed the door behind him. Hayden polished off his scotch and continued his blank stare, as his eyes grew heavier from the steady consumption of whiskey and guilt.

On the horizon, where the Atlantic Ocean met the night sky, the Nuwave sat inconspicuously on the unruffled waters. At a glance, just another pleasure boat in the busy Delaware Bay channel. But in the grand scheme of things, it was its precious cargo that set the vessel apart.

Jonas and Myra were sitting below, in the galley, playing cards. The child miraculously was the picture of health. Gone were all traces of the dreaded Crigler-Najjar Syndrome. There was richness to Myra's appearance. Her unnatural gold tinge was completely replaced by an alabaster complexion with perky cheeks of a rose color that accentuated her adorable dimples. The duo's quick witisms and playful banter were vital components of the bonding process. A relationship was developing, a mutual fondness, that would turn any mortal parent green with envy. Jonas and Myra lovingly attempted to make up for lost memories. It was a happy time; it was a dangerous time as well.

"War!" Myra erupted with excitement as she slapped the card down.

"Oh, no. But I only have two cards left."

"You lose." She said breaking into a little victory dance.

"Again? Wait, where's the rule book." Jonas protested, hiding his half smile, delighted by his daughter's offhanded prance.

Suddenly, the roar of a motorboat followed by static, sobered Jonas up. The smiling stopped as he peeked out of the porthole. It was exactly what he suspected, a Coast Guard cutter slowly pulling up next to the Nuwave.

"What's wrong?" Myra asked as she discontinued dancing. There was no reply from her father. He continued to watch the boat. "Father, what is it?"

Jonas held his breath as the Coast Guard cruised past the Nuwave without incident.

"Nothing." Jonas finally replied. "Everything is fine. I think we should get a move on."

He waited until the Cutter was a safe distance away, and then rushed out of the galley. The abrupt end to the game disappointed Myra as she collected the playing cards. Myra was more than willing to give her father a rematch, but it simply wasn't in the cards.

Jonas navigated the Nuwave over to the Cape May Lighthouse and docked it in front of the majestic seaside sentinel of brick and stone. He and Myra disembarked and as a precautionary measure, Jonas sunk the $400,000 48-foot Sea Ray. In a matter of minutes, the sea swallowed up Captain Jack's pride and joy, the stellar accomplishment of a rather unimpressive existence that no doubt had taken the fisherman a lifetime to afford. And although he felt a pang of guilt, Jonas chalked the Nuwave off as collateral damage; at least that's how it would read on the balance sheet. Jonas had Myra's safety to think about. Screw Captain Jack, he was, even in the best light, still a wife beater and at odds with his disenfranchised son.

Father and daughter climbed up to the lighthouse's lantern room where they enjoyed an unfettered 85-foot panoramic view of Long Beach Island and any impending dangers miles in advance.

"It's so peaceful." Myra said enchanted by the view. "So lovely. So—"

"Deceiving. Have you given any thought to what we talked about?"

"It frightens me, father. It scares me so."

"If you choose not to decide, you still have made a choice. Time is a thief, my child. They will eventually find us."

Myra refused to face the harsh reality. The inevitable, instead, twirled around like a tiny ballerina basking in the magic of the evening.

"Oh, I don't want to think about it. Only happy thoughts tonight, father. Please."

"Very well. What do you wish to talk about?"

Myra stopped spinning and smiled widely. "Mother. Tell me about my mother."

"Child, you don't need me for that. Your mother is in you, always."

Jonas touched his daughter's hand. Suddenly the entire top of the lighthouse illuminated with a lightness of being. The radiant onset of a nostalgic journey, told with all the wonderment in a child's heart, sparkled down Delaware Bay like a snowstorm in August. It was the memory of things to come.

CHAPTER NINE

"Could you be mistaken, Father Dougherty?" Inspector Cojocaru asked politely, authoritatively. But behind the cordialities, the chief of police in Cluj really wanted to suggest that Liam was out of his cotton-picking mind. Dougherty was perplexed, in deep thought as he stared off into the vast nothingness of the Carpathian Mountains. God help him, he was beginning to doubt what he was sure of. A convoy of police cars had converged on the scene. A swarm of local law enforcement was comparing notes in front of an oversized cottage. The cottage served as a museum of sorts, a popular tourist attraction. It was in all the brochures along side the Danube River Cruises and the Scarisoara, the 2nd largest European underground glacier, 90 miles southwest of Cluj. The signpost read: *Cluj Botanical Gardens.* Its proprietor, Miss Oana, late 50's wearing an expression of great concern, stood outside in a polka-a-dot housedress giving a statement to police.

"Sometimes, out here—"

"No!" Dougherty said firmly. "I am not mistaken."

"Are you certain it was on this very site? The countryside is extensive. Easily—"

"It was here. Khrushchev Manor was right here."

"But you can see for yourself, there is no such manor." The inspector pointed out as condescension inevitably reared its ugly head. Cojocaru's patronizing tone, however subtle, only fueled Dougherty's agitation. He began to ramble in place at first, and then Liam walked about, gesturing wildly. And if there were any questions as to Liam's state of mind, well, they were quickly being answered.

"There was a guardhouse to the left. He was watching television for Christ sake. And here, right here, a huge wrought iron gate with the initials AK...Now how would I know that? How could I know it?"

"As I stated, sometimes the woods can play tricks on the mind," the Inspector offered.

"It was here. Right where we're standing." Dougherty's insistence was not helping his case and a prime example of why defense lawyers seldom allow their clients to testify. "Right here, I'm certain of it."

"Well, as you can plainly see, it is not here any longer."

"And there, down that wooded passage was where Mr. Bianca and his son Aron put me in the wagon..."

The Inspector didn't doubt for a second that Dougherty was on the wagon. But it was becoming painfully clear that at some point during his travels, Liam had thoroughly and inexplicably fallen off the wagon. Cojocaru was thinking, *too much sacrificial wine with communion, perhaps?*

Once upon a time, there was a rickety suspension bridge where a most heinous attack took place; a cabbie lost his life while rocking out to Justin Timberlake's *Sexy Back*. Henric had a brother that lived in New York and the cabbie loved to watch the Sopranos, in fact, he never missed an episode. But that was a long time ago. And the evidence or lack there of suggested it was only in Dougherty's mind. Liam brought the police to that very same bridge; however, the crossing was far from dilapidated. Although it had seen better days, the bridge was completely intact, no lisping and minimum swagger. A far cry from Liam's assessment that the crossing was a hardy vibration away from total collapse. Dougherty stood, mid span, and studied the floor boards, the very spot that the cab's back tire crashed through, spun in place, sending up splinters of putrefied wood and rusted decay. The wood was pristine, equally sun bleached, matching identically with the rest of the bridge, ruling out any recent replacement, if Dougherty had any delusions of going there for an explanation. Liam walked the entire length of the bridge with inspector Cojocaru. He was hard pressed to find a single broken floorboard. And naturally, there were no traces of the assault and the ensuing blood bath Liam described to the inspector. Still, the police combed the bridge, unsuccessfully, for clues and spent rifle shells. Dougherty's attention turned to the bridge's suspension ropes. Liam looked up. He could still hear in his head, the awful whipping sound the ropes made as they unraveled and dropped into the river. Ropes didn't support the bridge at all; they were replaced in the late 80's and secured by steel reinforcement rods, making unraveling impossible and a worry of the past. To sever these babies, you would require a miter saw with an abrasive chop blade or a blowtorch. Can a tale get any taller? Sorry, Virginia, there may not be a Santa Claus, but there actually were roaring rapids under the bridge at some point, however that was sometime ago, quite possible during the Reagan administration, judging by the dry river bed below.

"Days ago the river was raging…," Dougherty told inspector Cojocaru.

"Father, there hasn't been a river here in years." Cojocaru resumed taking notes. "What was the name of the cabbie?"

"And you got this cab in town?"

Dougherty ignored him and continued to stare at the absence of water in disbelief. In Liam's head he could hear the pounding roars of the raging rapids, the sporadic gunshots. In his mind's eye, he saw the cab free falling off the bridge, slamming into the rock below. Dougherty heard the crash of the impact as the pronounced peak slammed through the bottom of the cab and out the sunroof. The blood stained windshield exploding from the force, skimming the rapids as a gyrating projectile. Henric's lifeless body snarled on the cab while it remained impaled on the rock as its doors simply washed away.

"Father, where did you get this cab?" the inspector repeated. "Father…"

The final stop on Dougherty's flight to fantasy was an abandoned rail yard. By this time, the concentrated police presence had dwindled, as did the balance of Liam's credibility. Inspector Cojocaru stayed the course, partly because it was his duty, the reason he made the big bucks, and also as the quintessential host, he felt an obligation to keep an eye on this obviously unstable individual, a stranger to his country. Dougherty believed his own bullshit with such staunch conviction; it tugged on the Inspector's heartstrings. He was quite patient with the priest while his colleagues tagged Liam a madman. The madman from the states.

Barely visible under the overgrown weeds were a double set of rusted train tracks that seemed to veer off to nowhere. This apparent dead end occupied the site that Dougherty remembered to be the Puravet property.

"So from the inlet this boy—"

"Lucian," Dougherty said.

"Lucian?"

"Puravet. Lucian Puravet."

"The boy brought you here?" Cojocaru asked by this time simply going through the motions.

"That's right."

"To these railroad tracks?"

"Yes—no. There weren't tracks here. There was an A-framed house with an adjacent barn right there." Dougherty pointed. "And sheep. Sheep everywhere."

Liam desperately looked around for some nuance of familiarity and then released a small, almost imperceptible chuckle in the stark absence of it, perhaps voluntarily, perhaps not.

"Please continue, Father."

"I met his parents, Sophie and Emile. Real nice people. Sweethearts. Genuine. Very hospitable. They saved my life…" Dougherty lifted his shirt to show the inspector his gunshot wound. Cojocaru's eyes dropped to Liam's bare chest, and then back up to Liam for an explanation. The priest realized that nothing he remembered so far had any validity or physical applications, why would the injury be any different? Sure, he was grimy and in desperate need of a shower and you didn't have to look close to see a few abrasions, a nasty black and blue, but no jiggered scar. No permanent testament to Sophie's seamstress abilities, certainly no indication that Dougherty had been shot. Or was he?

"...Emile was wheelchair bound. He has ALS..."

"What?"

"Amyotrophic Lateral Sclerosis. It's a disabling muscular disorder, a wasting away of motor neurons in the brain. Emile's chair was lopsided. It had a bicycle wheel on one side and the other tire was taken off a wheel barrel. How could I know such detail?"

"Tell me about the attackers?"

"They were hideous looking. Misshapen. Webbed feet. They grunted. They communicated by a series of grunts..."

"Can you be more specific?" the inspector asked.

"There were lots of them. They just kept coming. What do you want me to say?" Dougherty ranted. "Emile killed a few of the creepy bastards with his shot gun..."

The inspector heard enough, more than enough. Cojocaru's patience ran its course, and then simply expired like a New York City parking meter.   His fellow officers were accurate; Dougherty was a madman from the states and nothing more. He put away his trusty note pad. It was the Inspector's job to keep a written record of the facts; he wasn't an author of fiction or the fantastical.

"The man in the wheelchair with the muscular disorder, fought off a band of deformed killers?" Cojocaru reiterated, becoming more incensed at the absurdity of the story, the bombastic manner in which it was told, but ultimately it was the incredible waste of time that got under his skin.

"I realize how insane this must all sound…"

"No. You do not," the inspector said, mentally skimming through the legal statures in hopes of finding something to charge Dougherty with, even a misdemeanor would suffice. "Is there anything else you want to tell me, Father Dougherty?"

"The killers worked for Father Randall…"

Once upon a time, a priest was sent in the name of the Father, the Son and the Holy Ghost, to find the truth in a far away land full of falsehoods and deception…

Once upon a time, this priest was forsaken by his God and left to die in the hands of Satan, Lilith and their legion of demons…

And once upon a time, Terminus, the last scriptures of the bible were finally within Catholicism's reach. Or was it?

Dougherty doubted everything. Could it have been a cruel hoax, surpassing any elaborate David Copperfield like Vegas extravaganza? Now you see it, now you don't? A demonic slight of hand? The very thing Bishop Neely warned his students about in the seminary, "…in the spiritual world nothing is as it appears, nothing…," the Bishop exclaimed with a hardy Irish laugh that sent rolling ripples throughout his massive beer belly. But where did illusion end and reality begin, faith terminate and the road to perdition start…once upon a time?

Dougherty was on the next flight back to New Jersey quicker than he could say, *"peace be with you"*. In fact, Inspector Cojocaru saw to it personally. The Carpathian Mountains had gotten a bad rap since the 1800's thanks to Mary Shelley, even though Frankenstein took place in Ingolstadt, a city in Bavaria, Germany. But commonly mistaken for Romania by laymen and illiterates alike. So the local authorities didn't take kindly to rumors of monsters roaming the countryside and that included, but was not limited to, clergymen from the states, spewing shadowy tales of haunted castles and grotesque pygmy hit men, smack in the heart of tourist season.

The Archdiocese sent a car to Newark Liberty Airport, and gave the driver specific instructions, Father O'Donnell was to pick up Liam and bring him back to Monsignor Hayden's office directly, posthaste. O'Donnell was even asked to repeat the instructions in front of the elders and God, so as to avoid any miscommunications caused by his hearing aid.

Tired and disheveled, Dougherty sat fidgeting, across from the Monsignor as Hayden, silently skimmed through a death certificate.   He was still uncomfortably numb from the nonsensical story Liam seemed to be sticking with.   From Dougherty's perspective, the office seemed bigger and somehow it became longer.   There was a greater echo and Hayden's desk was that much wider, more intimidating than usual.   Even the Monsignor himself appeared distant, unwelcoming.   Dougherty hated being on the wrong side of Charles Hayden's favor.   Liam understood that he was in deep shit, maybe up to his receding hairline. He also realized that he disappointed many. Dougherty was unaccustomed to dropping the ball so miserably.   Failing was one of his least favorite things, its right up there with mom's pot roast and colonscopies.

"Anthony Randall has been dead for five years," the Monsignor said waving a faxed copy of the death certificate. "He died in Vancouver, British Columbia on April 26th, 2005 of an inoperable brain tumor. Father Randall was 48 years old."

"I don't care what that paper says. I know what I saw."

"Do you? Do you really? How's the drinking, Liam? Under control?"

"Alright, look, what do you want from me?"

"How about the pills?" Hayden probed. "Are we passed all that as well?"

"You came to me, remember?" Dougherty snapped back. "I didn't ask for this assignment. I was perfectly happy—"

"Wallowing in your own debauchery?"

There was an awkward pause as both parties stepped back from the heated exchange. The men were adults, friends for many years and colleagues for even longer than that, there was no reason things couldn't be worked out in a non-aggressive manner.

"What's next, Charles?" Dougherty asked in a sigh.

"That's an easy one. You wait for a call from Dean Wilson about the teaching job at Montclair State."

"What are you saying, Monsignor?"

"I'm simply owning up to my end of our bargain." Hayden shrugged. "I asked you to take a look at Myra, you did. This Diocese thanks you."

"What about the case?"

"There is no case. The child is gone. I have to believe that she is—no more."

"She's alive," Dougherty insisted. "I can feel it."

"My God, the emotional toll from this assignment must have been unimaginable."

"Its my nut, Monsignor. I can deal with it."

"Really? I was on the telephone with the Romanian police the better half of yesterday morning. Had to brush up on my

Romanian because I was too embarrassed to use a translator. Assassins with webbed feet? Demonic manors that don't exist? Shot gun totting paraplegics? I don't mind telling you the true miracle out of this mess, is that I got them to release you on your own recognizance."

"I address it all in my report. You'll have it on your desk by five o'clock."

"Don't bother." The Monsignor shook his head in disgust. "You've caused this Diocese enough shame."

"To hell with the Elders."

"On a personal note, because of your reckless disregard, my judgment has come into question."

"So you're firing me, Monsignor?"

"In a word, yes. Before they fire me."

"Charles, please. I have to find her. I owe it to Myra."

"You owe it to yourself to get well and defeat your demons."

"I'm trying, more than you'll ever know. In the meantime, I'm not going to stop looking for the kid." Dougherty pointed. "This case goes cold over my dead body."

"Know this Liam, you pursue this matter any further, and you'll be doing so without the cooperation of this Diocese."

"Yeah, well, what else is new?"

For a long moment, the Monsignor locked stares with Dougherty. And like a morning crap, Hayden didn't want to end the sit down too hastily, certainly not before all that needed to be said, was said and the inflamed bowels of the Monsignor's pent up frustration was emptied to his complete satisfaction. Hayden's eyes dropped down to his desk as he dove into the clutter of papers.

"Peace be with you, my son."

"And also with you," Dougherty echoed void of any emotion as he sprung up from his chair and walked out of the icy cold office.

A yellow cab emerged out of the stormy night, almost phantom-like in the sudden deluge of rain, and cautiously made its way down the quiet tree lined street. It's headlights bounced off the poor visibility as it pulled up in front of Dougherty's apartment building. Liam paid the driver with a fifty. The cabbie winced; he knew it was going to be trouble do largely to the fact that his shift just started. No matter how many times the driver sifted through the till, a frayed cigar box discriminatingly stashed under the passenger seat, he could not make change. So Dougherty over tipped the cabbie in loving memory of Henric. Liam got out of the cab and struggled up the steps with his cumbersome luggage. He opened the lobby door with his key and squeezed into the tight entrance suitcase first. The vestibule was dimly light, due to a fluorescent bulb broken in its fixture. *How does an easy fix, remain so chronic?* Dougherty wondered and after maintenance or the absence of maintenance was brought up during a recent tenants meeting with the landlord promising sweeping improvements. The remaining bulb looked to be on its last leg, maybe total darkness would prompt some action, maybe. The lobby was wall papered with flyers and building announcements that the Wednesday night Mah-jongg game had been moved to apartment 4B. And then there were the sounds of a multi-unit dwelling, a baby crying, Michael Kay calling the play by play for the Yankee game, And of course, no evening would be complete without Mr. And Mrs. Gonzales arguing. The couple were born in Princeton, spoke perfect English, yet they fought in Spanish, it was a trip. Dougherty stopped at the cluster of mailboxes and grabbed his overstuffed mail. He briefly thumbed through it, as he half listened for a score of the game, the mail consisted of advertisements mostly. Liam was numb from the events of the past 72 hours and his pace exhibited it as he sluggishly crept up the stairs. The unexpected sound of glass shattering from inside the Gonzales' apartment. *It was good to be home.* Dougherty thought reflecting. *It was good to be alive.*

Liam walked into his apartment and flicked on the light. He tossed the mail on his desk, the letters and circulars scattered, knocking over an ashtray filled to the brim with crushed butts. Dougherty reached for his trusty bottle of Jack Daniels, but no luck, it was bone dry. He turned the bottle completely upside down, inside out, hoping to draw an unfinished drop, trying to muster up that smidgen of residue before it morphed into evaporation. But every trace of the whiskey had been previously consumed. Liam sat on his sheet less bed, kicked off his shoes while rubbing the jet lag from his face. On the night table, the answering machine was blinding with a degree of urgency as Dougherty reached over and played his messages.

"Tuesday 9:51 AM," the robotic voice sounded followed by a beep. "Hi, this message is for Mr. Dougherty. This is American Express calling—"

Dougherty deleted the message.

"Wednesday 3:03 PM," the robotics continued as an elderly woman's sweetness filled the musty apartment. "Happy Birthday, dear. Just a reminder, in case you forgot that you have a mother in Brooklyn and she would really love to hear from you. So give me a call. Hope all is well. Okay. Bye now."

Dougherty smiled before deleting the message.

"Friday 5:30 PM," still more robotics, then a man clearing his throat. "Yes. Good afternoon, my name is George Wilson.

I'm looking for Liam Dougherty. Monsignor Hayden suggested I call regarding a teaching position at—"

Dougherty quickly, almost angrily deleted the message as the machine's red indicator light vanished; there were no more messages. Involuntary, Liam's attention turned to his desk, at the 8x10 photos of Myra and her markings in various stages of development. The pictures were tacked to a corkboard with certain aspects of them highlighted and notations made in bold red. Below the photographs, ghosts of Christmas past...maps with longitudes and latitudes circled. Dougherty defiantly turned away, then quickly looked back. The child taunted him like a poltergeist. His eyes were drawn to the photos like tiny magnets. In his mind's eye, Liam saw a montage of photographs in rapid succession causing him to leap up from the bed, charge over to his desk and wildly rip the pictures off the cork board, ripping and tearing at them.

"To hell with the Diocese and Hayden...," Dougherty hollered, caught in the propulsion of his helplessness, he knocked all items, related or not, off his crowded desk top with a swift sweep of his out stretched arm. "To hell with this case...!"

There was a rumble of thunder; a flash of lightning illuminated the return of Arthur Shield.

"Now that's my boy," he said, leaning unperturbed against the wall sill. "That's the Liam that I know and love. On a roll and totally out of control."

"Oh no. I'm done with you, Arty. We said our goodbyes."

"You obviously missed me. Look at yourself." Arthur motioned to the wall mirror with caked on soot.

"Get out!!!"

"How many more lives, Liam?   How much more destruction can one man cause?"

"I denounced Satan. I tried to do good…"

"Good? You've been a very bad boy. You damn near dogged that poor peasant woman in Romania. What was her name, again?" Arthur struggled to remember.

"I tried to help Sophie."

"Help?   By slipping her the high, hard one?" Shields grabbed his crotch. "You wiped out her entire family. True, her husband had an expiration date, but he still had a few good months left."

"And maybe none of it ever happened."

"And the kid, Lucian…He was as pure as the driven snow. Now he's all gone."

"What do you want from me?"

"I want you to stop whining like a little bitch. Man up! Do the right thing. You know those pills you've been saving for a rainy day? Well, brother, in case you haven't noticed, it's pouring." Arthur walked toward Dougherty with a mischievous swagger as more flashes of lightning exploded in his background. Shield pointed to the desk, the drawer slid open, the exposed pills rattled inside. "Take em, Father Dougherty. End your pathetic life!"

"Myra?"

"Do you want to ruin her too?"

"Get behind me Satan!!!" Dougherty shouted digging deeper into his reserves for the energy, the will to resist.

"We have 72 virgins waiting for you on the other side." Arthur whispered directly into Liam's ear. "Nah, just kidding. The virgins are earmarked for suicide bombers like me. There's nothing on tap for hophead ex-priests. Truth be told, virgins are boring. I'd prefer strippers and porn stars. But I don't make the rules. I just follow them."

Arthur had worn Dougherty down. Once again, Shields had driven him to the brink of sanity, granted it was a short drive. Emotionally depleted, Dougherty collapsed on his desk chair, swiveled toward the drawer and removed the pills.

"Maybe you're right," Liam conceded as he opened the bottle and stared at his fate.

"I'm always right. Just a swallow away from everlasting calm."

More thunder. Another streak of lightning brightened the room, spotlighting Arthur long enough for Dougherty to recognize that Shields had no reflection in the mirror, and then realizing further that Arthur Shields was just an illusion, born of a prostrated conscience, and the crap that Liam ate on the plane. Without hesitation, Dougherty threw the pills against the wall, shattering the bottle into a dozen pieces.

Under the I 95/I 395 interchange, off Conway Street near Oriole Park at Camden Yards, the Seville Diner was open for business and business was booming. The diner was first opened in 1952 by Pat and Ethel Frawley, and quickly became a permanent fixture in the tapestry of downtown Baltimore. A trucker's paradise because of its easy on, easy off proximity to the highway. The Seville was one of Maryland's most beloved greasy spoons and home to the *Fat Cat*, two all beef patties, chopped up, packed into a pita and complimented by the toppings of your choice.

Inside the busy eatery, the commotion level was deafening, from the crappy country ballad on the juke box, to Jodie the waitress bouncing from table to table refilling coffees with a piping hot pot of decaf in one hand and a pot of regular in the other. No one could hear themselves think, the perfect atmosphere for a pair of unlikely fugitives, and that sat just fine with Jonas, who subscripted to the theory, *the loudest one in the room, is the weakest one in the room.* Jonas and Myra were trying very hard to go unnoticed as they occupied a booth next to a bay window that overlooked the parking lot. Jonas was wolfing down his breakfast grand slam with extra bacon and a side of grits. Myra on the other hand, poked at her food rather unenthusiastically.

"How are your pancakes?" Jonas asked. "Blueberries enough for you?"

"I guess."

"What's wrong, sweetheart?"

"Nothing?"

Through the window, Jonas noticed a police cruiser pull up behind a parked Chevy Impala. Trooper Harris radioed in the license plate number.

"Could have fooled me, Myra."

"Just thinking about school."

"What about it?"

"I'm nervous. I mean, what do they do there?"

Once again, Jonas' attention was diverted to the parking lot as Trooper Harris parked his cruiser and squeezed out of the car, adjusting his pants while his gun belt still hung significantly below his enormous beer belly. The lawman finally straightened up, and lumbered into the diner. Trooper Harris was a mountain of a man, the closest thing to a big foot sighting that side of I 95. Assuming the cops got a hit, that the Chevy was indeed stolen, and presuming fatso called for back up, Jonas calculated the response time by local snapper heads patrolling the boondocks to be slightly over two minutes give or take. Plenty of time for a father and daughter to wrap up their table talk before all hell broke loose.

"They teach. Fun stuff like reading, writing and arithmetic."

"Boring." Myra folded her arms in protest.

"These mortals embrace the mundane. Lucky for us, anything more advanced is beyond their comprehension."

"But you already taught me to read and write. Why do I have to go?"

"We've discussed this, to assimilate. Their society mandates that all children your age must be in school. So off we go. Think I'm happy about it? I'm going to miss you a great deal young lady." Jonas reached over and pinched her cute button nose. "Now finish your blueberry pancakes before I steal some."

Jonas leaned across the table and kissed his daughter. Myra looked down and saw that her pancakes had vanished and then materialized on her father's plate.

"Hey…"

"I warned you." Jonas laughed. "You snooze, you lose."

"Give em back!"

"Want another milk?" Jonas asked sliding his plate over to Myra and holding up his coffee cup in a futile attempt to attract some resemblance of service. "I need a refill. Have you seen our waitress? Terrible service in this dump."

Myra nodded, digging her fork into the pancakes and dragging the pancake through a tidal wave of maple syrup. Jonas looked toward the counter and spotted his waitress talking to Trooper Harris. It was a good bet that they weren't comparing her C-section scars to his stretch marks. No sir, turned out "Jizm" Jodie, that's what the good old boys at the trailer park affectionately called her, was all about service, community service as she pointed out Jonas to Sheriff Buford T. Justice without hesitation.

"Should have gotten those hot cakes to go." Jonas motioned to Myra. "Ready?"

Myra took a final fork full of her pancake as Jonas threw down more than enough money to cover the tab. Father and daughter slid out of the booth quickly. Myra winced from a friction burn on the back of her thighs as her shorts rode up and flesh met leather. The duo walked toward the exit where Trooper Harris confronted them.

"Excuse me sir, is that your brown Impala outside?" the Trooper asked reeking of coffee and donuts.

"Afraid not," Jonas replied avoiding eye contact.

"Waitress says it is."

"My daughter needs to use the facilities, Officer."

"Jodie, would you escort this pretty young lady to the rest room?"

"Damn it Clifford, I got tables to mind." Jodie stomped her foot. "Ain't no windows in the bathroom anyhow if that's what you're thinking."

"Do it anyway, please. Thank you, Miss Jodie."

Jodie followed Myra into the ladies room under protest.

"What's the problem officer?" Jonas asked.

"The Impala has been reported stolen. License and registration please."

Reluctantly, Jonas removed his wallet and handed the trooper his identification. Harris' eyes dropped down.

"This is a library card…"

When the trooper looked back up, Jonas was gone. Harris rushed into the dining area, the only logical place Jonas could have run. Every booth was filled with an identical Jonas and Myra. All commotion stopped. The diner became weirdly quiet. The only sound in the joint was Jimmy Buffett's "Margaritaville" playing on the jukebox and the Trooper's heart palpitations as the father/daughter impostors turned to look at him in chilling synchronization. The look-alike faces were distorted, oblong and yet compressed. One side warped, the other perfectly normal, dimples intact. It was as if Harris was looking at reflections in a fun house mirror, the same reflection multiplied by 50 impersonators. The longer the Trooper stared, the more the faces sagged and took on a ghoulish, almost liquefied appearance. "Jizm" Jodie bolted out of the ladies room. Startled, and thoroughly spooked, the Trooper turned to her, placing his hand on his gun. She couldn't find the words, but lucky the waitress didn't have too, Harris understood by her look of puzzlement that Myra had disappeared as well. The Trooper turned back to the dining area; the counterfeit Jonas and Myra were gone as unexplainably as they had appeared. The sound of normalcy returned. Now you see it, now you don't. A demonic slight of hand? Of course, how could anyone forget, "…in the spiritual world, nothing is as it appears, nothing…" Words to live by, words to die for. Harris heard the screeching of car tires. He rushed over to the window and watched the Impala peel out of the parking lot, appropriately leaving a black cloud of debris, burnt rubber and confusion in it's wake.

Trooper Harris ran out of the diner so clumsily, pants drooping and his extra large boxers showing, he nearly fell over his own legs. Sooner rather than later, Harris would have to do something about his weight. It was becoming increasingly more embarrassing. His fellow officers at the station house reinforced Harris' desk with cinder blocks, co-workers can be merciless. Getting into shape had been the Trooper's New Year's resolution two years in a row, envious of his sister in law Janice, who dropped 17 pounds on Nutrisystem. He stuffed himself back into his cruiser and chased after Jonas with sirens blaring. The Impala splashed onto the treacherous stretch of Route 713, coined *"Snake Road"* by the local teenagers with a propensity for drag racing. The Impala hit a ridge at speeds well above the posted 35 miles per hour and took flight. Upon landing, its belly scraped the road with a clang, losing a hubcap on impact in the bargain. Sparks belched out from the car's undercarriage as it wildly bounced around before finding a suitable northbound lane. Trooper Harris was right up Jonas's ass, in hot pursuit and practically kissing the Impala's fender. Fatso was a native, certainly no stranger to *"Snake Road"*, and he effortlessly negotiated the road's irregularities when allowed him to remain uncomfortably close. As familiar as he was, Harris was still nervous, sweating profusely in fact, "...*in a high speed chase, anything could happen. The slightest distraction can prove catastrophic...*" that warning didn't come from Bishop Neely at the seminary, that invaluable caveat was issued by Captain Tommy Thompson, chief instructor at the Maryland Police

Academy. Trooper Harris kept both eyes glued to the narrow byway, while he called ahead for back up.

"I'm in pursuit of a stolen brown Chevy Impala—heading north on 713...," he screamed into the radio.

The impala made a quick left, a hard right, screeching from the two-wheel skid as another hubcap flew off. The trooper's reflexes were soft; he swerved to avoid it a little too late. The hubcap hit the front end of the cruiser, flipped back and rolled unevenly up the hood and safely over the windshield. The Chevy over compensated for a sharper, ascending turn and fishtailed recklessly out of control across route 713 and into the lane of an on coming tractor trailer. The truck immediately sounded its horn, an instant communiqué, "*smarten up or die!*" It was an unmistakably jarring warning of the impending doom to the driver of the Impala. Apparently it worked, the car veered away just in time, but the near miss caused the Chevy to side swipe the side of the mountain. Its passenger window shattered as the Impala spun back across the roadway and careen off a guardrail or two. The Trooper stayed the course, maneuvering out of the Impala's destructive path. Harris accelerated and then jammed on the brakes. He repeated the procedure several times during the duration of the chase, sometimes utilizing both feet for the desired results.

"No sir.   Not on my highway," the Trooper ranted.
"You're not going to get away with this crap on my watch, no
sir. And here comes the cavalry…"

In the distance, a pair of police cruisers turned into each
other and formed a roadblock. The Troopers, both men much
thinner than Harris, withdrew their weapons and assumed a
marksmen stance outside their respective vehicles. The crazy
ride was coming to an end, winding down in front of the
officers as the approaching Impala slowed, a steady stream of
steam was surging from under the hood. The Chevy was
certainly wounded, evidenced further by the loud clanking noise
emanating from its wheel base, it sounded as if someone had
trapped a handful of screws in a coffee can and was incessantly
shaking it. The car came to a complete stop a dozen or so feet
from the roadblock. Trooper Harris' cruiser skidded on to the
scene, with a boisterous screech. Anxiously, the Trooper got
out of his car, as quickly has his hips would allow without the
assistance of any lubrication, and moved toward the Impala
with his gun leading the way.

"Get out of the car!!!" Harris hollered. "Hands on your
head!!!"

The doors on both sides of the Chevy flew open. Trooper
Harris paused in anticipation of the perpetrator, or perpetrators
to surrender. This was going to be an impressive text book

arrest, it had to be, the judgmental eyes of his fellow officers were on poor porky Harris and he was well aware that you never got a second chance to make a first impression. Interestingly, on the police report, the excessive time allotment would come into question, but it wouldn't matter, this was Harris' baby, it was his call.

"I said, let me see your hands!!!" he shouted.

Still, there was no sign of movement. The Impala simply sat, idling. The other Troopers surround the car and cautiously peeked inside. Trooper Harris' worst fears were realized, the Chevy was empty. Once again, Jonas and Myra had given the police the slip. The arrest would make the textbooks all right, but for all the wrong reasons.

"Father, I really do have to go to the bathroom." Myra's voice rang out, driving the Troopers crazy.

"We'll be home soon, honey." Jonas' reply fueled the flames as the Troopers spun around in place. Each cop looking in different directions for a physical body to match up with the voices. Unbeknownst to them, the voices were coming from inside their very own heads. Now you see it, now you don't. A demonic slight of hand? Of course, how could anyone forget, "…in the spiritual world, nothing is as it appears, nothing…"

CHAPTER TEN

Absent of any fanfare, no cake was offered up and not a single candle was blown out on his behalf, but it didn't prevent Liam Dougherty from turning 44 last Thursday. Liam wasn't one to worry about age, he didn't stress over his own mortality, more pressing matters filled his analytical mind, or they had until Monsignor Hayden discharged him of all his duties and removed the weight of the world, the spiritual world from his buckling shoulders. But Dougherty was beginning to notice some changes that came with age, beyond morning joint pain and the occasion strands of hair in his ears, it was an about face of emotions. Feelings of melancholy were subtly beginning to creep into his tough guy facade. For example, lately and for the first time in his life, Dougherty had been feeling lonely, irrelevant and that's what prompted his trip into Brooklyn. A diversion, regardless of how brief, might be just what the doctor ordered. He'd see some old faces. It would be good for the soul, and it couldn't hurt. Liam didn't get back to the old neighborhood very often. It was a trek that included New Jersey Transit to Penn Station, a switch to the D-train, ride to the Avenue U stop and then a cab to his mother's house. That day, however, Dougherty thought it might be therapeutic for him to walk from the train station, at the very least it would be cost efficient eliminating a cab fare. From the moment he stepped out of the train station, Liam's eyes drifted off to a happier place and time, remembered, as always, in nostalgic black and white. As memories flooded through him, Dougherty returned to his childhood, suddenly he was 10 years old again and walking up the busy, sun drenched avenue passionately holding his AM radio, listening to Elton John. Everything was from the 1970's, from corduroy pants with bell-bottoms to Member's Only jackets. 1970's cars populated the roadway, from Dodge challengers to the Oldsmobile Cutlass. A favorite smell caught his attention; something good was in the air. As Liam passed Josephine's Bakery, now a used tire store, he waved to Josephine as she placed a fresh tray of assorted cookies, chocolate Napoleons, cherry jelly top and rainbow sprinklers, in her window. Good old Josephine had a mole above her upper lip with unsightly hair growing out of it every which way. She also had the largest breasts, pound for pound, of any storeowner on the avenue. Her tits were bigger than basketballs and some water floatation devices. Obtrusively, in the middle of the block stood the Mayfair Theatre, now a Kingdom Hall for Jehovah's Witnesses. Once a movie palace in its glistening prime with a colossal art deco marquee framed with twinkling lights, the marquee extended to the curb, providing shade from the sun to a pair of neighborhood wise guys in leather jackets and slicked back hair. Vincent "Vinny Cool" Montebello and

Tommy "Toupee" Sorvino were hanging out next to Vinny's Cadillac Coupe De Ville. Their current whereabouts; well Vinny was deceased, killed in a gang related knife fight, God rest his misguided soul, and Tommy "Toupee" was serving 25 years to life for the kidnapping and murder of a union official's daughter.

Dougherty turned the corner of his old block, and in his mind's eye he saw the stark image of Sylvana, the prostitute that lived above Charlie's drug store. The attractive brunette was hanging out of her window and shaking out her dust broom. She appeared to be doing it in slow motion. Sylvana was exactly as Liam recalled, skimpily dressed and untouched by time. Barely visible was her tattoo of the Italian flag above her right breast. The prostitute spotted Dougherty and waved excitedly.

As Liam made his way further down the block, the sounds of yesteryear intensified. The laughter, the arguing, the yelling was all part of a soundtrack that made up his world. Then there were kids, faceless, shadowy, almost phantom-like frolicking under an open fire hydrant. Those same children were also huddled in the street playing Skully. They appeared again in a neighbor's alley having relay races. And a final time as the kids fanned out over the entire block playing Ringolevio and chanting a chorus of "Ringolevio 1-2-3, 1-2-3, 1-2-3!!!" and a single shout of "free all!!!"

Favoring the element of surprise and forgoing a conventional front door entry, Dougherty snuck around to the back of his mother's house instead where he found Irene Dougherty fussing around in her impeccably maintained garden. Irene was fast approaching 80 years old. She was a rough looking broad, the female counterpart to James Cagney, only with a constant tremor. The woman had a pasty complexion due in part, to her deteriorating circulation. Her continually tired expression was the direct result of the hardships she endured raising two children alone on a phone company employee salary. Irene's glassy bloodshot eyes were post cataract and magnified behind thick black-rimmed bi-focals. God blessed Mrs. Dougherty with a terrific full head of white hair, strikingly white, Santa Claus white.

"Hey lady, what the heck are you doing bending?" Liam asked walking over to her.

"I have no problem bending," Irene said surprised. "It's the straightening that is the tough part."

Irene stretched out her hand and Dougherty helped his mother up with her back and neck cracking ever inch of the way up. She immediately hugged and kissed her son. It seemed to Liam that her hugs were getting tighter, more prolonged. Was Irene happier than usual to see Liam or was she relieved to see him?

"This garden will be the death of you."

"From the soil we are born, and into the soil we shall return. What a pleasant surprise. What can I get you, Liam?"

"I'm fine."

"Let's sit. I just made some ice tea." Irene ushered Dougherty over to the patio, where they sat at a table under a polka-a-dot umbrella, tilted slightly to the east for optimum shade. The outdoor furniture was a bit tuckered-out. It was the same set Liam bought his mom for mother's day over a decade ago, and although chipping in spots, the wicker had held up surprisingly well against the harsh Brooklyn winters.

"So how have you been?" Irene asked.

"I'm OK."

"Not very convincing. You look like crap."

"The job I guess."

"Oh yes, the work of our Lord is endless. There are a lot of sinners out there."

"Amen."

"Did Kathy call you?"

"No. Why? Is everything alright?"

"She's having a boy. They found out a few weeks ago."

"Really?" Dougherty smiled. "That's terrific. I'll have to brush up on my curve ball."

"Did you get my message?"

"That's why I'm here."

"Sure as hell took you long enough. Guess people don't come to Brooklyn unless they have to…"

"You OK?" Dougherty could sense that she was hiding something by her sarcasm, but he just couldn't put his finger on it. So he pushed, maybe not hard enough? "Mom is everything alright?"

Irene stared off and for a fleeting moment thought about telling Liam of her recent trip to Mount Sinai and all the unpleasantries of her MRI, like the hospital gown that was three sizes too big, the constant draft up and down her spine from a room where there were no windows, a technician who looked a hell-of-a-lot like their Uncle Murray, and of course, the dastardly results of the test, given to her by Doctor Izzo with his deepest, most heartfelt sympathies. But that was news for another time, when her condition began to deteriorate. That afternoon, Liam would be given a plethora of information to process. It was long over due, a startling fact about his father, before it was too late. Irene believed that memories were as transient as vapor. She wondered, now more than ever, in light of her life concluding affirmation, "*if no one was left to remember, did it actually happen?*"

The radio caught Irene's attention as she reached across the table and pumped up the volume.

"…This Senator Clarkson. She is a great speaker. I hope she runs for President. I'd like to see, in my lifetime, a woman hold that office," Irene said.

"She couldn't screw things up any worse, I suppose." Dougherty paused and pressed a final time. "What's wrong, mom?"

"You know there isn't a day that goes by that I don't think about your father." She affirmed with a smile.

In Dougherty's mind, he immediately flashed back to when he was 10 years old, it was in that very house, in the kitchen, his father Paul Dougherty, sat at the table nursing a beer. Liam was on his favorite seat in the entire world, his father's lap and stared up at his hero with wide-eyed wonderment. It was abundantly clear from his expression, that Liam adored his old man as he hung on his father's every word.

"…Life is tough pal, but it is not impossible. Keep your wits about you and you'll do fine…," Paul advised as he took another swallow of beer and looked at his son with a haze. That perpetually dazed expression, a shell shocked, blue collar stare that resulted from 60-hour workweeks and the hopelessness of the lower middle class.

The recollection ended and Dougherty was back in real time with his mother.

"Me too. I think about Pop as well"

"Funny thing about loss, people will tell you it hurts less over time. It doesn't. You just have to make do. He was crazy about you. So prideful. You were the apple of his eye."

"Did you really call me here to talk about Pop?"

"Sometimes I think you cheered him up more than his medications."

"Medications? What medications was Pop taking?"

"Anti depressants, mostly," Irene replied, still unsure if she was doing the right thing, tarnishing her son's memory of his father. "Loads of anti depressants…"

"What are you saying, Mom?"

Irene Dougherty began with a quivering bottom lip that would travel throughout her body before the story was finished. Once upon a beautiful, fall morning, a younger Irene was setting the table for breakfast. Present were Liam, 10 years old and his sister Katherine, a few years his junior, both were buried in their notebooks finishing their homework before the 8:15 school bus. Like older siblings, Liam loved to break his sister's chops and that morning was no different. He glanced over at her homework and laughed.

"That's not long division," Liam said with a slight lisp that eventually dissipated when he got into middle school. "Writing the problem out with bigger numbers doesn't make it long division…"

"But it's taking up the whole page and the page is long…," Katherine defended her work.

"That would make it big division, stupid ass."

"Mom, Liam said the A-word."

"Liam Patrick Dougherty, I will not allow that kind of language in my house."

"I'm sorry Mom," Liam mumbled lowering his head.

"Apologize to your sister immediately, young man." Irene turned toward the stairs and hollered, "Paul, breakfast is ready."

"I'm sorry, Kathy…," Liam suddenly smirked. "I'm sorry you're a stupid ass."

"Mom, he said it again," Katherine cried, surprised at her brother's brazen disregard for the law of the land. "Are you going to wash his mouth out with soap?"

"Soap is too gentle a punishment. I'm going to brush his teeth with a brillo pad." Irene said as she walked to the stairs holding a pot of scrambled eggs and shouted up.

"Paul, breakfast is getting cold. Where is that man? He is just exhausting," Irene muttered to herself. "Liam, go get your father, please. Tell him we'd like to eat breakfast before lunch."

Liam scooted upstairs, climbing the steps two at a time. Irene sat at the table and began filling Katherine's plate.

"Honestly, that man will be late for his own funeral."

A young Liam walked whimsically toward his parent's bedroom.

"Pop…Pop, Mom wants you…" He called out.

Liam heard the water running and as he walked closer, he could see water gushing out from under the bathroom door, spreading all over the hallway carpet. The water had a red tinge to it. Liam stepped down onto the wetness with a loud slosh as he put an ear to the door and knocked.

"Pop…?" He shouted as his happy-go-lucky outlook ended and his instincts, although not fully developed, took over. Liam attempted to open the locked door.

Downstairs, back in the kitchen, Irene watched Katherine shovel her eggs into her mouth and rolled her eyes.

"Slow down," Irene instructed. "Nobody is going to take it away from you."

"The bus?" Katherine was barely able to get out, juggling a mouthful of eggs.

"You've got plenty of time. More bacon?"

"Yes, please."

Irene lifted the frying pan over her daughter's plate. A red drop hit the eggs and splattered over the home fries. Before any of it could register with Irene, another drop fell, followed by another and another, in rapid succession, from the ceiling.

"Stay here!!!" Irene fed the order to Katherine and rushed upstairs with increasing concern.

"Pop won't answer." Liam stood puzzled with his ear pressed firmly against the door. "I don't think he can hear me."

"Go downstairs and make sure your sister gets on the bus!" Irene hurried over and tried the locked door, noticing the blood at her feet. Liam simply stood there watching, waiting. He didn't know why, he was a victim of instincts that were sharpening quickly, too quickly.

"Do it Liam!!!" Irene screamed "Do it now!!!"

Liam ran off, charging down the stairs like a thoroughbred at the stretch. Seeing his mother's eyes bulge out of her head when she yelled, scared the crap out of him, a sight like that can scar an impressionable lad. It was an image that would stay with him for a while, not nearly as long as if he would have actually walked in on his old man. Irene waited until her son was safely downstairs before she retrieved a dusty spare key from the top of the doorframe. With a trembling hand, she unlocked the door Irene and her mature keen instincts had a real bad feeling and she wasn't disappointed. She rushed in to the bathroom and found a very pale Paul Dougherty in the bathtub, staring vacantly. His arms extended in front of him, bobbing up and down on the surface of the water from the gush of the flowing faucet. Both wrists had been slit right down to the bone, any remaining blood spurting sporadically. Irene stood frozen in horror, her hand covering her mouth so she would not scream at the grisly discovery.

Concluding her story, Irene appeared desensitized, while Dougherty was paralyzed with emotion. He was afraid to move, afraid to breath. Irene noticed a stray cat approaching her garden.

"If you go near those melons, so help me, I'll capture you and sell you to Lucky Noodle take out," she shouted at the black and white kitty.

The feline continued its defiant path toward the garden until Irene stomped her feet. Irene's legs cracked and the cat scampered away from the indistinguishing noise of bone meeting cartilage, rather than her heavy footsteps.

"I thought he died of cancer." Dougherty asked, still flummoxed by the revelation.

"Inoperable cancer of the spirit."

"Why are you telling me this?"

"When I couldn't reach you, I phoned Trenton. Spoke to Charles Hayden. He said you were on leave indefinitely due to personal issues."

"The monsignor had no right…"

"He had every right, Liam. And I'm grateful. I just wanted you to be aware of the history."

"Why didn't you say something sooner?"

"Didn't want anyone playing the blame game," Irene confessed, keeping a close eye on the damn cat, who had perched itself on the top tier of the fence and was waiting Irene out. She couldn't stay out in the backyard all night, not in this heat. "Besides I felt guilty enough for all of us."

"Mom, we could have helped."

"You were on a need to know. And now my dear, you know." Irene sipped her iced tea. "What are you going to do now?" Do you have anything lined up?"

"Those who can't do, teach Mom," Dougherty sighed. "I think I'm going to be a teacher."

Life on the run was beginning to take its toll on Jonas and Myra. *Now you see em, now you don't*, came with an enormous price tag. No parent worth their salt would want that existence for their child, regardless of how intellectually advanced the kid happened to be. So it was no surprise that the sleepy little town in Virginia would appeal to the Paynes. It seemed to be a suitable cover to settle down and take a stab at normalcy. It could work as long as father and daughter immediately set up privacy boundaries, with rules that would have to be obeyed without compromise. Rule # 8, optimum anonymity; any small talk with neighbors would have to be curbed. Rule # 2, for a successful life on the lam; avoid being on a first name basis with anyone. Nothing more inviting than a cordial wave, or a nod of acknowledgement in passing. Conversation, no matter how frivolous encouraged diarrhea of the mouth, and diarrhea of the mouth revealed particulars, idiosyncrasies, in which a person, if so inclined, could create a profile or composite. Apartment complexes were ideal for such isolation; tenants were generally antisocial and kept to themselves inside their one or two bedroom slice of life. The peepholes in their double enforced doors scrutinized potential visitors, rejecting or embracing them into a controlled environment of their own design where they lived happily ever after in a cold detached bliss. The Ashford Arms Apartments seemed the perfect fit for the Payne's aforementioned criteria as well as being germane to another guideline; it was affordable. Apartment 2B was spacious with hard wood floors throughout and a pretentious view of the Rappahannock River. Jonas and Myra walked around the unfurnished space with the realtor following closely behind overselling the unit.

"The maintenance fee is very reasonable for this type of apartment. I assure you," the realtor said with a mousy voice that could conceivable annoy the dead. "And please keep in mind, your utilities are included in the rent. Sorry, you're relocating from…?"

"Jersey," Jonas kept it short and sweet.

"What brings you to Fredericksberg?"

"How are the schools?" Jonas asked side stepping a reply by answering a question with another question. Mindful of rule #5 in the "on the lam" survival guide, all realtors were yentas. It's in their nature and why they gravitate to the field.

"How old are you, dear?" the realtor turned to Myra and faked a smile.

The child ignored the question all together and simply stared at the realtor stone faced, taking her cue from the original parental rulebook, "*no talking to strangers*".

"She's nine," Jonas answered.

"Let see, you have Hugh Mercer Elementary. It's one of the finest in the state," the realtor paused. "Is it just the two of you or is there a Mrs. Cartwright?"

Jonas and Myra looked at each other and silently agreed. Apartment 2B had one other convenience besides a two year lease that the realtor wasn't aware of, but had she known, she would have talked it up till nausea, the place came with the promise of stability. And for an exhausted Jonas and Myra, fresh from the road, it was impossible to put a value judgment on a peace of mind.

"We'll take it," Jonas said.

In the following days and weeks, the Payne's lifestyle had stabilized just as they had hoped. Father and daughter were now as boring as vanilla ice cream, as routine as bypass surgery. Jonas cherished his time with Myra. The pair was inseparable, so it was no great surprise that on the first day of classes, Jonas would walk Myra to the elementary school, if nothing else, to lend moral support to his daughter and to present her with a soothing influence. They leisurely made their way up the shady suburban block, as squirrels frolicked across the neatly manicured lawns moist from the morning dew. In their foreground, a precession of cars pulled up to the school and unloaded their kids. Myra tensed up in anticipation of joining a crush of children grades K thru 6$^{th.}$ As they collected and eventually funneled through the school's gate, Jonas and Myra faded into the crowd, but stopped at the main entrance. He handed Myra her backpack.

"Ready?" Jonas asked.

Myra unzipped the backpack and prepared for a final once over.

"Ready."

"Notebook?"

"Roger," she confirmed fumbling around inside.

"Two number two pencils?"

"Roger."

"Box of crayons?"

"Roger."

"And your mid morning snack?"

"Roger," Myra said nervously looking in her backpack. "Where are my glasses? Father, I forgot my glasses."

"Sweetheart, you're wearing them."

Myra quickly reached up and confirmed her father's assertion.

"Oh, yeah. Roger that."

Jonas smiled. Myra smiled back until she spotted Freddy Ferguson, the school's custodian approaching. Freddy was in his mid 50's, schlepy and dirty looking. There was something about this guy, something off, something Myra couldn't quite put her finger on. Then again, it could conceivably have been nothing, an over reaction, a false reading, an inaccurate impression thanks to the whirlwind of emotion and angst brought on by the dreaded first day of school. And although being nervous was a normal kid thing, her elevated levels of anxiety were not. Freddy Ferguson frightened Myra, case closed. The smile dropped off Myra's face as she stepped closer to her father. Freddy smirked at her as she walked past him.

"What is it, honey?" Jonas asked.

"Nothing."

"Nervous?"

"No," she lied.

"It's OK to be nervous. But it's all going to be OK. I promise."

"Bye father."

"Remember, I'll meet you right here at 2:45."

"K. Love you."

"I love you more," Jonas assured her.

Myra kissed her father and scooted into school. Every father, in all walks of life, across this glorious country, felt the proverbial knot in the pit of their stomachs when sending their kid off to school for the very first time, and Jonas was no different. His eyes welled up with tears and for a long moment he thought he was going to cry. He cowardly scampered off, seemingly inconsolable.

Rule #3 for being on the lam applied more to Jonas. In order to ingratiate himself with the human world, and to fully absorb small town America, he needed to land a menial job, preferably one that didn't ask too many questions. And if references were impossible, a stellar first impression was imperative. Jonas wasn't afraid of hard work and he never met a motor he couldn't fix. He was truly gifted that way and had magic hands when it came to repairing his tractor. So Jonas Payne and Clint's Automotive seemed a logical fit. The garage was looking for help and Jonas happened to be looking for work. It was a no brainer. The joint was jumping with some cars up on the hydraulic lifts, others not. There were mechanics scurrying around from every direction, rolling tires, under hoods and eating their lunch. A centrally located boom box was blasting a pulsating Latino beat that only served to fuel the chaos. Jonas entered and walked up to the closest grease monkey he saw.

"Boss around?" Jonas asked over a spasmodic symphony of electric screw guns.

The mechanic remained under the car and didn't even look up. He simply pointed to a tall gentleman in the back of the shop. Jonas dodged and darted through the disorganization until the tall gentleman addressed him.

"Picking up or dropping off?" the boss asked, marking up the nudie calendar behind him. It was a notation, something about the delivery of a Honda part coming in next Tuesday. "Either way your not suppose to be in the work area."

"Are you Clint?" Jonas inquired.

"Clint's been dead for five years. Who are you looking for?"

"Work."

"Oh, OK. For a minute I thought you were an inspector. OSHA has been a real pain in my ass lately." The boss attempted to wipe off the oil with a rag greasier than his hand, but decided to abort the handshake all together, or save it for another time. "I'm Tommy."

"Ben. Ben Cartwright. Glad to know you."

Rule # 12, was a given. If you were really serious about remaining anonymous, never, ever give your real name. Make one up, something easy to remember. Try to avoid being overly ethnic, and be sure you matched the ethnicity that you had selected, because there was no turning back. As a last resort you can always pick from a movie or television show. A word to the wise, if you go that route, by sure to select a character from an obscure foreign film or a TV program from the Stone Age. Ben Cartwright happened to be Lorne Green's character in the 1959 series "Bonanza". Jonas recently saw an episode on free cable in one of the many extended stay motels he and Myra frequented of late.

"Know anything about cars, Ben?"

"Only everything."

"Confidence. I like that. As long as it doesn't turn into arrogance." Tommy remarked. "Been a mechanic long?"

"Half my life." Jonas answered.

"What did you do for the other half?"

"Worked *for* a mechanic."

"Ever been in the joint?"

"Joint?"

"Jail. Ever been in jail?"

"Not yet."

"Good one. Not yet," Tommy laughed, taken aback by Jonas' fearlessness. "We can always use a good man around here. Always so swamped. A man who complains about business won't be in business for very long."

"In that case, I'd love to interview for you at your convenience."

"So it's around quitting time, and widow Willis pulls in with her 1975 Dodge Dart. The car is her pride and joy. Her baby. Bought it new back in the day. It's been acting up, but it's her only means of getting her weary 88 year old bones around town. Finish the scenario…"

"I escort Mrs. Willis to the waiting area, assuming there is a waiting area…"

"Assume away."

"…Pour her some coffee, at her age, I'm thinking decaf, climb under the hood and bang out her problem regardless of how long it takes." Jonas presented the hypothetical without flinching, as he took his best shot at a stellar first impression.

"Congratulations. When can you start?"

Ordinary was good. Ordinary worked for the Paynes. Their apartment worked for them as well. It was Jonas and Myra's sanctuary from the ills of the world, a world Jonas believed to be completely and incurably insane. Three nights a week, they would order in. The rest of the time Jonas cooked. Nothing elaborate, chicken cutlets were quick and easy, his spaghetti and meatballs usually got rave reviews. Sometimes, he'd prepare a salmon when the supermarket had it. There wasn't anything super about the local market. It was simply a glorified 7-eleven. For the Paynes the conventional sit down dinner preserved quality time and created a forum for both father and daughter to vent, address each other's concerns and or just plain kibitz. That night, Jonas tried to get fancy and cook beyond his scope. He overcooked a tender piece of London Boil into a blackened scrap of shoe leather. Wolfgang Puck he was not. It was all so new to him, and like everything else, Jonas was learning by trial and error. He over compensated for his culinary inadequacies by making sure the cupboard was well stocked with quick fixes for life's little oops…

"How was school today?"

"Denny was being mean again," Myra frowned contentedly eating her dinner.

"Do you want to talk about it?"

"Nope."

"Honey, if you don't like the way someone treats you, speak up!" Jonas instructed. "You should let them know. Don't be afraid to tell them how you feel."

"I did. I told Denny."

"And what did he say?"

"He said, 'poop' to me."

"Excuse me?" Jonas put down his fork.

"I said Denny, I don't like the way you treat me. And he said, 'poop to you, Myra' Can you imagine the nerve? Denny said 'poop' to me."

Jonas looked away. His knee jerk reaction was to laugh, but he knew it was no laughing matter. There were times, too often lately, when Myra desperately needed her mother's nurturing advice and this was one of those intimate moments. Jonas felt so inept, so incapable. He could do little more than silently beg Anna to help him find not only the words, but also the right words.

"Sweetheart, sometimes when a boy treats you mean, it may be because down deep he really likes you and he doesn't quite know how to express himself."

"Father, did you ever say poop to mom?"

"No. Clearly I'm not as romantic as Denny."

"What's romantic?" Myra tinted her head inquisitively like a new puppy reacting to an unfamiliar sound.

Once again, Jonas discontinued eating and grimaced, horrified by the can of worms that he may have inadvertently opened.

"And what would you like for desert, young lady?"

"Can I have Easy Mac for dessert even if I had it for dinner?" she asked.

"I think that's called seconds." Jonas scooped more food onto her plate. "You really like your macaroni and cheese, huh?"

"It's Freddy Ferguson's favorite too."

"Who's Freddy Ferguson? Another boy in your class?"

"No. Freddy is old and creepy. He works at the school. I think he's the janitor. He's weird. Freddy spooks me."

"Stay away from him," Jonas said firmly, trying to ascertain if this guy was a real problem or an exaggeration in a child's mind. "If he bothers you, tell one of the teachers. Understand?"

"OK."

"And tomorrow, when I walk you to school, I want you to point this Freddy the janitor out to me. Alright?"

The next day, Jonas was late for Myra's dismissal because of a hypothetical realized, except it wasn't widow Willis' Dodge Dart, it was the transmission on Reverend Doeskin's flat bed Ford that kept him at work longer than expected. When Jonas finally arrived at the school, on foot and sweating through his shirt, hordes of children were already pouring out of the main entrance in a euphoric gush of freedom. The kids habitually rushed into their parents out stretched arms, double-parked mini vans and waiting cars. The air was filled with cheers and laughter. It was all routine, typical, except there was no sign of Myra. Jonas checked his watch; it read 2:53 pm.   She was 8 minutes late and counting. The crowd thinned, Jonas became visibly nervous. His daughter was usually one of the first smiling faces out the door. Jonas looked up and down the block and panned the grounds for Myra and as the last of the students dribbled out, he became frantic. He verified the time; it was now 2:56 pm. Myra was over 10 minutes late, even a bathroom pit stop would only account for half the time, tops. Something was wrong, something was terribly wrong. Jonas had a bad feeling beyond a father's paternal instincts, his keen intuition was not of this world and proved to be accurate 101 percent of the time. Jonas spiraled into a manic state. His breathing became labored as implausible thoughts raced through his head, could he have somehow missed Myra? If you had, where would she go? Why wouldn't she simply wait for him? And is it possible she's right under his nose and he doesn't see her? Jonas knew the answers to those foolish interrogatories, but he retraced his steps anyhow. It was now 3:01 and still no hint of Myra. She was now 16 minutes late and her father, rightfully so, began to fear the worst. He looked up at the big blue heavens, closed his eyes and soundlessly prayed, *"Anna, please do not forsake our daughter, please,"* Jonas begged of his late wife, hell bent on entering the school building. Suddenly, his prayers were answers; Anna would never let him down. A sigh came to him slowly as Myra came charging out from behind the school. Jonas' relief was short lived as his daughter ran into his arms, crying hysterically.

"What is it? What's the matter?"

"It's Freddy Ferguson," Myra replied through a series of sobs and with tears streaming down her face.

"What about him?"

"I know you told me never to do it, but I did…"

"What did you do?" Jonas asked pointedly. "Tell me. It's Ok, honey. Calm down. What did you do to Freddy Ferguson?"

"I changed him."

"Where is he?" Jonas questioned, remaining calm.

"Are you mad?"

"I'm not mad! Please, focus! Tell me where Freddy is?"

"He ran off behind the school after—I—I changed him."

"Show me. Take me to him!!!"

Myra ushered her father into the back of the school as fast as her little legs could take them. Jonas and Myra stopped and looked around. Just peaceful green countryside as far as the eye could see. There was no sign of anyone on the grounds or on the jungle gym, just empty swings and monkey bars. But the unnatural stillness warned Jonas and his ghoulish instincts that something was amiss, tranquility begged of wickedness afoot. And sure enough, a squealing of sorts breached the calm and then all hell broke loose. The shrieking was accompanied by intermittent banging that seemed to be emanating from a shed next to the creek. The wailing intensified, as did the banging to the extent that both became wildly out of control and sounded like a bucking bronco bouncing off the walls inside the shack. Wood on the side of the shed cracked from the force and glass shattered as Jonas caught a glimpse of hoofs and animal-like hind legs as it kicked out an entire window. More glass was smashed. Jonas sat Myra down on a tree stump for a heartfelt father/daughter chat.

"Did Freddy Ferguson touch you?"

"No."

"Did he say something inappropriate to you?" he asked trying to understand.

"No."

"Then why did you do this?"

"He had bad intentions," she confessed.

"Honey, you can't punish someone for what they are thinking. Their thoughts are private. They belong to that person."

"I'm sorry, father. Please, don't be mad."

A high pitched whining, almost human sounding in nature, rang out from the shed, followed by sobbing.

"Wait here! Don't move!!!"

Rule # 6, in order to fully assimilate in society, avoid at all costs, turning a creepy pedophile into a more hideous monster than he already was.

Jonas walked up to the shed, a shack saturated with ungodly howls of flamboyant agony. He slowly reached for the knob and the wider he opened the door, the more sunlight spread across the unspeakable. As long shadows were cast, he got another peek at the abomination; its misshapen head and long razor-like claws, immediately took a swipe at Jonas as he stepped in. Freddy Ferguson was no more, just an unpleasant memory, in his place, a monstrosity with narrow red eyes that flashed repeatedly as it hugged the shadows, standing on all fours with a donkey-like torso.

Outside the shed, Myra heard the rustling, and the commotion of the creature's death noises. They were so deafening, the child had to hold her ears for what seemed like an eternity, but was simply a matter of seconds. It all ended rather abruptly with more broken glass, a series of thuds, and a final vile scream. At the sound of silence, peace and tranquility returned, and Myra embraced it like a long lost friend. The worst was over. Now it was just a matter of making amends with good old pop. The door to the shed opened and Jonas emerged blood soaked, and pretty pissed off, but otherwise, no worse for wear. He picked his frightened daughter up by the arm and quickly fled the scene of the crime.

Later that night, back at their two-bedroom sanctuary, cracks were beginning to show and vulnerability was seeping in as the reality of being outcasts stormed the castle. Myra spent most of the evening holed up in her bedroom, embracing the darkness and steadily crying over the events of the day. Jonas elected to remain at the kitchen table and polish off yet another bottle of wine. Much like Novocain during a root canal, the Chardonnay had an equally numbing effect on the cavity in his soul. Jonas wasn't exactly sure, was it *drown your sorrow and feed self-loathing* or the other way around? He always got the adage confused with *feed a cold, starve a fever.* Either way, after another glass of vino, nothing would matter much. Jonas closed his bloodshot eyes, clasped his hands together and addressed his one and only with the utmost humility.

"...My love, my angel, give me the strength, I beg you. Give me a sign, Anna. Show me what to do..."

CHAPTER 11

The classroom at Montclair State was packed to the rafters, not because the course was riveting by any stretch of the academic curriculum, but because it was a prerequisite for Anthropology 201. Dougherty stood in the center of the room, lecturing to yawning students that would rather be anywhere else. The Theology course, *The Absence of God in a God Fearing World*, met once a week for 10 weeks, providing matriculating undergraduates 3 relatively easy credits, and for the professor, it offered a steady paycheck and dental insurance.

"…Talk about injustice of biblical proportions? The plight of Judas immediately comes to mind." Dougherty's voice echoed in the large room and off the blank stares. He was as bored as his students, and if there was a way to nap while lecturing, Liam would have discovered it. "Here's a guy whose role on the great stage was for no other reason than to drop a dime on the Son of God. This poor bastard was born, betrayed Jesus and then killed himself. Talk about short changed. What did this misunderstood soul ever do to deserve such a destiny?"

The buzzer sounded after the rhetorical question, and mercifully ended the class. Students sprung up faster than the speed of light, collected their belongings and quickly filed out.

"Finish up chapters 1 and 2 by next week," Liam shouted, ignoring the passing moans and groans from some students. "And don't forget our quiz on the 28th."

Dougherty walked back to his desk and gathered his books. He looked up at the empty classroom and saw Myra sitting front and center. He was paralyzed by the vision.

"Imagine the plight of a man that doubts what he is sure of?" Myra said sweetly. "A man whose role on the great stage is for no other purpose than to betray himself."

Dougherty stared at the child, incapable of a reply. It had been months since Myra's abduction. The memory of her haunted him relentlessly, he could think of little else. Liam's mental health was slipping, deteriorating rapidly with illusion spilling into reality more frequently. As if some higher being was having their way with him.

"I don't get it. Arthur Shields killed a few babies and you quit the priesthood. A little bump in the road in Romania, and you give up on me."

"I tried to make sense of it." Dougherty's eyes welled up with tears. "You're not real."

"My father says the worst thing you can be in this world is…unfinished."

"I suppose he's right."

"Don't give up on me, Liam. Please."

"God, I've missed you, child."

"And I you," Myra smiled.

"Tell me what you want from me?"

"A picture is worth a thousand words."

"Be my guest." Dougherty said holding out the chalk.

Myra accepted his invitation. She walked over to the black board and drew a funky looking door. Dougherty opened the door, inside was the Federal Building in downtown Trenton. Myra reached for Liam's hand.

"Coming or not?" she asked warmly.

Now you see it, now you don't. Dougherty was apprehensive, knowing full well that "…in the spiritual world, nothing is as it appears, nothing…" It came as no surprise that Liam followed Myra on that fateful night. He would have chased her anywhere for the answers. Nothing was worse than not knowing. An inconclusive story wasn't much of a story at all. Dougherty needed closure more than the air that he breathed, and the vodka he consumed. For his trespasses, he got his ending.

Liam took Myra's hand and together they stepped through the black board, into a world beyond the child's chalk door.

Dougherty found himself alone in a crowd on the streets of downtown Trenton. Myra had simply faded away or perhaps she never was. It didn't really matter; this was one journey Liam

would have to take solo. The clues were out there. Everywhere
he looked fragmented pieces of truths floated about heckling
him, daring Liam to a *mensch*. It was time to connect the dots.
He owed it to the child and to himself to see this enigma
through to fruition regardless of the dangers, regardless of the
outcome. In the nucleus of his crippling doubt, one thing was
certain, crystal clear, the answers began in the Federal Building.
Dougherty slowly climbed the daunting steps of justice, but
couldn't help being concerned about how he would be
perceived? He assumed the investigators read his report, was
his creditability intact? Did he ever have any believability in the
eyes of the Feds? At the very least, they would have to hear him
out as a professional courtesy. Both Dougherty and the G-men
had the same objectives, the preservation of truth, justice and
the American way.

Inside the building, there was a labyrinth of disorder, a
supervised anarchy of endlessly long corridors of marble upon
marble. There were rows of unmarked doors identical in every
way. A blur of pinstripe suits walking the halls, are seemingly
familiar with the layout. He got lost twice and had to stop
someone for directions. They directed him to the third floor,
dedicated to investigations. That department was a scaled down
version of pandemonium, with telephones ringing off the hook
and agents buzzing around in their cubicles. Dougherty

stopped a shapely female Fed, she pointed across the room. He made his way through the chaos over to Agent Bigger's cubicle. Biggers was behind his desk, buried in his computer with his back toward Dougherty.

"Agent Biggers?"

"Yeah."

"I'm Liam Dougherty..."

The agent stopped what he was doing and turned to Liam.

"...From the Trenton Archdiocese...," Dougherty added just to clarify.

"I know who you are. What can we do for you, Father?"

"I was in the neighborhood, thought I'd inquire about the progress in the abduction of—"

"There's nothing to report, Father. But we remain—"

"Foolishly optimistic?"

"Can I get you something, coffee? Tea?   A fifth of Absolute?" Biggers fired right back.

"I was hoping to take a look at Myra's file."

"I've been over that file 100 times. Everyone up here has."

"Surely a fresh pair of bloodshot eyes couldn't hurt," Dougherty offered.

Agent Bigger's impulse was to go with his gut and deny Dougherty access. But to what end? Who would benefit by refusing Liam and throwing him out on his drug induced ass?

Certainly not the missing child. Whether Biggers liked it or not,
he and Dougherty were on the same side. It just made sense to
serve their common cause.

"Have a seat."

Dougherty pulled up a chair. Agent Biggers spun around to
a cabinet and retrieved a file boldly marked case #2011. He
placed it in front of Dougherty. Liam skimmed through the
police reports and then focused in on the photographs, 8x10
pictures, mostly in black and white. There was a photo of the
damage to the roof of the Archdiocese. Another picture of
Myra's bedroom at the Diocese, emphasizing the twisted door
completely torn off the wall.

"And these pictures?" Dougherty inquired.

"Taken inside Jonas Payne's house in Lancaster," the agent
said glancing over.

Dougherty came across another photograph of the outside
of Jones' farmhouse. Liam paid particular attention to what
appeared to be three streaks of light hovering over the roof. He
slid his finger over the marks, and scratched at the glossy finish
with his thumb just to discount any imperfections in the picture.
The streaks remained, and upon closer examination, were lined
up in an almost wishbone configuration.

"Anything leap out at you, Father?"

"Liam. Please, my name is Liam."

"See anything I should know about, Liam?

"Won't know definitively until I take a look. Tell me Agent Biggers, do you believe in demons?"

"I read your report, Father."

"My reports are not worth the paper they're written on."

"The Monsignor thinks you're burnt out."

"And you, Agent Biggers? What do you think?"

"Oh, I know you're a head case." The Fed admitted, without pulling any punches. "But I still have a missing kid on my hands."

"So then, can I bum a ride?"

Jonas Payne paced in the hallway just outside of his apartment. He was enjoying his Chesterfield immensely, taking long drags and filling his lungs up with the smooth menthol flavor until his chest burned. *It hurt so good.* He thought waving away the smoke rings. The door opened and Myra popped out in her Winnie the Pooh pajamas. Jonas quickly hid the cigarette behind his back and tried inconspicuously to smack down the clouds of tobacco. He was unsuccessful. They somehow managed to put the Freddy Ferguson matter behind them and it was life as usual. As horrifying as it was for the Paynes, they were not the victims. It was poor Freddy the janitor that never knew what hit him. However, his gruesome death was not in vain, it served as a rude awakening for Jonas. He would never allow himself to be complacent again, there was simply too much at stake.

Jonas always encouraged his daughter to have an open dialogue with the Lord, knowing that he could never be present for any of it.

"Did you say your prayers?" Jonas asked.

"Yes," Myra said, affirming that the coast was clear.

"That was quick. All your prayers?" Jonas pressed. His tone an octave shy of implying that she was fibbing.

Myra walked back into the apartment. Jonas attempted to flick the butt out of the open window, but missed. He got lucky as the cigarette hit a pane of glass and rolled off the windowsill, dropping into the night air without a trace. Jonas caught up with his daughter in the living room.

"Said an extra prayer to Mom, thanking her for helping me through the first week of school," Myra commented throwing herself on the couch.

"Your mother always use to say, 'when life brings you to your knees, pray'."

Myra reached for the remote, finally digging it out from under one of the pillows. She pointed it at the television and was about to check in on her favorite TV show, but her father had other ideas.

"Hope you're not thinking about watching TV. Time for bed, miss. You have school in the morning."

"Father, tomorrow is Saturday."

"Just teasing," Jonas laughed. "You can sleep in. But it *is* late."

Disappointed, Myra dropped the remote and slowly got up from the comfortable couch. Jonas escorted his daughter into her bedroom. She had a typical little girl's room, pretty and pink, Myra's favorite color.

"Father, what did mom look like?"

"She was beautiful," Jonas reminisced fondly with a smile. "Breathtakingly beautiful."

"Wish I had a picture of her."

"So do I sweetheart. I'll see if I can dig one up. Until then you're just going to have to take my word for it. Your mother was an angel."

"Read to me?" Myra asked climbing into bed.

"Maybe tomorrow night. Pleasant dreams, kiddo." Jonas tucked his daughter in. Myra wiggled and snuggled until she found the right spot in the lumpy second hand mattress.

"Love you father."

"I love you more," Jonas assured Myra as he kissed her forehead. He walked out of the room and shut off the light.

"Can you leave the light on?"

"Myra, there is nothing in the dark that isn't there in the light, you should know that. We're living proof of it."

"Just until I fall asleep. Please, father."

Jonas smiled and turned the light back on.

"Pleasant dreams, my love."

"You won't forget about mom's picture, will you?" Myra asked fearful that her father might have already dismissed it. However, the contrary was truth, Jonas could think about nothing else other than Anna's photograph. So intense was his obsession, he was about to break the number one rule for a successful life on the lam…NEVER, EVER RETURN TO THE SCENE OF THE CRIME!!!

It was a crisp country evening, not a false note in the rustic tapestry. Humid, but not stifling. Not only was Jonas Payne's farmhouse lit by the crystalline glow of an odd shaped moon, the entire hill top was galvanized by it.

The sound of crickets chirping in true falsetto could be heard in the thickness of the night. The mashing of rocks interrupted the nocturnal glee club, as the government issued sedan crept along the winding dirt road. Above the farmhouse, there were three spectrums of light lazily lingering over the residence. And as the sedan pulled up to the house, the trio of lights seemed to awaken. They floated upward, separated, and then rocketed across the sky like shooting stars before vanishing into the balmy twilight.

Agent Biggers and Dougherty got out of the car. The agent reached into the backseat for a flashlight and ushered Liam up the front porch. Biggers tore away the crime scene tape that stretched across the door and threshold. Then he barreled into the door shoulder first. The brittle wood crackled in half before breaking into pieces. The men walked into the house as the withered floorboards creaked under their feet. Naturally, Biggers' flashlight conked out and pitch black engulfed the duo.

"Maybe we should have waited for daylight?" the agent said slapping at the flashlight until illumination returned. "I know, there's nothing in the dark that isn't there in the light?"

"Wanna bet?"

Dougherty proceeded into the living room as the floorboards squeaked louder, more pronounced. He stopped at the make shift shrine to Anna Payne. The agent walked over throwing some light on the hundreds of photographs plastered haphazardly on the long wall. Liam put on his glasses, leaned in closer to the pictures, and began to study them.

"Interesting," Dougherty nodded. "All these Kodak moments are only of Anna Payne. Where's Jonas?"

Absorbed by the preponderance of snapshots, neither Dougherty nor the Fed noticed a menacing shadow that passed over agent Agent Bigger's car, which was immediately preceded by a loud thump in the night.

"We didn't turn up a damn thing on Anna Payne—" The agent was interrupted by a rowdy crash. Jonas made a grand entrance ripping the remains of the front door apart. Everything in the house that wasn't nailed down rattled. Startled, Biggers dropped his flashlight. It staggered across the floor with its rotating light flickering, throwing illumination everywhere and nowhere at the same time. The agent reached for his gun. Jonas, a room away, held out his hand and lifted Biggers off the ground. Jonas' eyes flipped back, only the whites were visible. They rolled in their sockets like a pair of undersized cue balls causing the agent to twirl ballerina-like until the gun dropped out of his hand. Jonas raised his arm and willed the agent head first into the ceiling. There was an explosion of dust and debris. But Jonas wasn't finished playing just yet, moving his outstretched arm right to left, let to right, he sent Biggers effortlessly gliding through the air and bouncing off the walls with the velocity of a racket ball in motion.

"Enough!!!" Dougherty hollered. "You're killing him."

Jonas stopped as he slowly came to his senses. Jonas was just as startled to find intruders in his home. The otherwise pacifistic farmer simply got caught up in the moment. He stood motionless while Agent Biggers remained suspended in mid air. Jonas slowly lowered his arm and the agent fell to the floor unconscious. Dougherty rushed over to the Biggers.

"He's going to need a doctor," Liam said checking for a pulse.

"You're the priest?" Jonas asked walking into the living room. "The one my daughter says is kind?"

"And you're not just some local shit kicker, are you? I want the truth this time, Mr. Payne?"

"I am simply one of many that have fallen," Jonas explained, looking at the pictures of his beloved Anna. "Isn't she lovely?"

"Myra's mother?"

"Yes," Jonas confirmed. "My angel."

"How is the child?"

"Curious about her mom. And rightfully so." Jonas gingerly ran his fingertips along the photo. He closed his eyes, savoring his wife's likeness.

"What's going on here, Mr. Payne? What are you?"

"I'm a father. I'm Myra's dad. And a damn good one. Before that I was simply a husband."

"And before that?" Dougherty hesitated to ask.

"I was lost. Berith commissioned a select group of us to do what we do best—"

"Berith the demon?"

"Oh Father, he is much more than that. He is the Duke of Hell with 26 legions of demons at his command. You do not say no to Berith."

"Are you suggesting that you are a—?"

"The mission was to corrupt one of your world leaders. This isn't about the mission. It's about the treasure I found along the way. Anna was sent by her people to protect this head honcho. And I was sent to destroy him."

"Her people?" Dougherty asked.

"Your team. It was a divine decree."

"So Anna was an angel?"

"Direct from heaven. I earnestly attempted to corrupt and demoralize the mark. Anna gracefully countered with kindness and compassion. I became enchanted by her goodness. The beguiled had become bewitched. For decades I repressed my feelings of humanity, gentleness, hope, and yes, love. Those emotions are forbidden and impossible for someone of my nature to feel. I could resist no longer. It overwhelmed us. My actions would be a slap in the face that Berith could never forgive. I know he'd have his minions scour the earth looking for me...for us." A single tear escaped Jonas as he became lost in recollection. He told Dougherty about their origins. How Jonas and Anna hid in the last place on earth the demonic posse would look, Lancaster, Pennsylvania. A Dutch wonderland of harmonious bliss, from the picturesque town square to its quaint amphitheater. A community steeped in religious tradition, off the beaten path and completely out of touch with the amenities of life, and yet it oozed with appealing charm. An uncomplicated place where the streets were filled with the Amish riding around in their horse drawn carriages, gentlemen would tip their hats and ladies frequented antique candle shops at an outdoor village called Kettle. The sun seemed to shine a little brighter. Everyone appeared to have more love in their hearts, exemplified by permanent smiles as they pranced around tending to their own affairs. A true spirit of commonalty existed, gushing with an abundance of humanity. It was the perfect cover for entities that were far from human. And the best part about this Mayberry USA, the Strasburg Railroad ran through it.

It was on a warm summer day, in the green pastures of the Pennsylvania countryside, the receptacles were first noticed, quite accidentally by the entities. Jonas Payne and Anna Alberts were very much in love. Their feelings for each other were never in question. However, Jonas was Amish and Anna was not, and that was that. Jonas' father Jonathan, the Amish community called him Yonnie, was a God fearing, stubborn man who resisted change with every fiber of his being. So it came as no surprise that when his only son, the apple of his eye, asked for his blessings to marry Anna it was met with an emphatic nod of disapproval. In fact, Yonnie not only forbade the proposed union, but any further mention of it under the Payne roof. But Jonas was a man in love, with raging hormones; he fearlessly and valiantly fought for his happiness, confiding in Elder Daniel from the congregation with the hopes of enlisting his help in changing Jonathan's mind. The strategy failed miserably and young Jonas was not only thrown out of his house, he was shunned by the church as well.

Jonas didn't need family or his God, a faith he once held dear to his heart, he had his most prized possession, Anna. The couple exchanged vows in front of a store bought preacher in an empty chapel, a town away in Intercourse, PA. Only the bride's great aunt Mary Lou attended, and she slept through the 20-minute ceremony slumped over the first seat in the front pew. The woman had fallen victim to a stroke a few months back and never fully recovered.

The couple moved into Jonas' place, a farmhouse that was willed to him by his grandmother some years back. Jonas tirelessly worked the field to support his new bride. The newlyweds lived in marital bliss for a while. Their self-imposed exile from friends and family, coupled with Anna's inability to conceive, was beginning to take a toll and a sizable chunk of the couple's sanity. It was an emotional roller coaster that went on for years. Anna, who was not necessarily a religious person, began to believe that the Lord had brought blight down upon them for their sins. But the true culprit, the real scoundrel that drove them to the brink, was the fact that both Jonas and Anna never made peace with such total isolation. It was the seclusion, the consummate abandonment that attracted the *entities*. It was exactly what they relished, the main ingredients for an unpretentious life. The real trick was keeping it from Anna. She would have done everything angelically possible to prevent the couple's final act of love. It occurred in the bedroom, on a fateful autumn afternoon. Jonas and Anna were sitting on the bed. She was crying into her husband's loving embrace, an everyday occurrence of late. And routinely, Jonas tried his best to comfort his wife. He reached into his bag of tricks, like he did a thousand times before, he fumbled around inside his satchel of encouragement, antidotes and plans for the future, but this time Jonas came up empty. He simply had run out of a reason for being.

That old adage, *nothing lasts forever* applied to misery as well. So without any further adieu, Jonas walked out of the bedroom and returned with his pals Smith and Wesson. He pointed the revolver at Anna and put two .38 rounds in her head before turning the gun on himself, firing a single shot into his temple. Jonas fell to the floor, as did the smoking gun. At long last the Payne's had found their elusive calm, their eternal peace. Or did they? It was all so tragic. It was all so sudden. It was all too perfect, a golden opportunity for the *entities*. Suddenly, Anna sat up on the bed, eyes open and staring hazily at the mosaic bloodbath that was once her brains, and now decorated the wall. It was a reversal of sorts, praise the Lord, although the Lord had nothing to do with it. The bullet holes in her face were getting better, going away like a bad case of acne. The discoloration of her gunpowder-singed complexion was lessening as tendons and nerve endings were mysteriously fusing together expeditiously under a cascade of gooey discharge. Particles of blown away cheekbones replenished as the gaping holes in her face began to refill. Jonas slowly got up. He too was looking much improved, the entrance wound had scabbed up nicely and the only evidence of his suicide was a missing patch of his hair just above his ear where the bullet exited. The couple examined themselves. They tested their new body parts, as wonderment over came them. Jonas and Anna stepped up to each other. He was hesitant to touch, almost fearful of breaking her. Jonas gingerly caressed Anna's shoulders and closed his wanting eyes in a gush of exuberance. At last he possessed the power of touch and his newborn flesh sizzled. At long last, he owned the ability to smell Anna's aroma, it was so intoxicating, so addictive, he could have held her forever, or until the fires of hell froze over. The couple locked in a perpetual embrace, filled their lungs up with sweet liberation, as a smile came to them slowly, finally. Their spanking new bodies were flawless receptacles, well equipped to host all the passion in their hearts. Demon and angel lost in desire. Good and evil united and a hot breath away from partaking in human pleasures. Unheard of, and yet it was done.

Jonas abruptly stopped, ending his story of forbidden love with an unintentional cliffhanger. His supernatural Romeo and Juliet, had no conclusion, the outcome was still unwritten. The demon smiled a final time at his wife's pictures.

"She was my life."

There was a sudden whistling in the wind. Jonas turned toward the crushed door, and understood immediately.

"Are Berith's people still looking for you?" Dougherty asked.

"They have already found me," the demon answered disappointedly as he heard the approaching footsteps. "Quickly, there is little time." Jonas removed some pictures off the wall. He jotted down Myra's address on the back of one of them, and then handed the collection to Dougherty. "A little girl should know where she gets her beauty. Please, see that my baby gets these."

"Is there something I can do to help?" Dougherty asked with urgency in his voice.

"Fall back into the shadows. Say nothing. Lilith must not see you."

"Mr. Payne, maybe we can make a run for it out the back." Dougherty suggested with that same sense of urgency now turning into desperation. "There's got to be a way to stop this...?"

"The book is the only way to stop it," Jonas reaffirmed. "You must not give up on finding Terminus. Protect my little girl, priest. Trust no one! Trickery and illusion are at the demons beck and call."

"I'll take care of Myra. You have my word," Dougherty pledged as he soundlessly stepped back into the shadows.

Lilith appeared in the doorway looking more like a corporate CEO than the queen of the succubus. Her jet-black hair was pulled back in a tight bun and she was seductively dressed in a black pinstripe pantsuit, custom fitted to show off her exquisite figure. Lilith's round frame glasses took the conservative librarian look to the umpteenth level. Two male cronies appeared next to her, also dressed to the nines, in expensive suits of European design. Lilith grinned at Jonas, there was a verbal exchange, some Latin, the rest demon gibberish. Dougherty barely heard it cowering in the corner of the room, but if he had to venture a guess, Lilith was undoubtedly expressing a sense of relief that their cat and mouse escapades had finally come to a diabolic culmination. Lilith turned and walked out with Jonas following closely behind her. Dougherty peeked out from the darkness and watched the demons walk down the hilltop and out of sight. *Now you see em. Now you don't....*

Dougherty drove frantically through the night, to be in Virginia by morning. His motives were not exclusively to grant a man's final request, although Liam couldn't be sure that Jonas received the death penalty for his flagrant disobedience. Whatever the punishment, Dougherty was certain that leniency was no part of the equation; it simply didn't exist in the demon dichotomy. Liam was also quite sure that regardless of the penance, Jonas didn't regret a moment of his marriage. The love that he and Anna shared was transcendent, not of this world. Judging by Jonas' look of adoration, and the way his world brightened up by looking at Anna's picture, Dougherty was convinced that he'd gladly repeat the cruelest of torture for just one more kiss. Liam had selfish reasons for going to the Ashford Arms that morning. He missed the child desperately.

Dougherty walked up to apartment 2B and once again, he took out the photo of Anna and checked the address written on the back. It was a perfect match. *This was the place* he thought and nervously knocked. Myra answered the door and smiled almost immediately.

"Liam, I've been expecting you."

Dougherty was both surprised and relieved at how incredibly healthy the child looked. Liam choked on a swell of emotions as a king sized knot formed in his stomach.

"You were? Great. I hate to disappoint anyone. How've you been, pal?"

"I'm making French Toast. Would you like some?" Myra asked.

"I kinda had my heart set on blueberry pancakes."

"My favorite."

"Did you actually start cooking?"

"Nah. I'm not allowed—not without my father," she shrugged. "I just got out the pan and stuff. Have you seen him?"

"What do you say we go out for breakfast? We got a lot of catching up to do."

Myra got excited, and then realized it was a bit premature for celebration, she needed permission to leave the apartment. "I gotta make sure it's alright with my father…"

"Your father knows."

"Really?"

"It's cool."

"I'll get my keys." A smile returned to her as she ran into the apartment.

Dougherty stood in the doorway. He noticed a DVD of "The Lion King" playing on the television. Myra raced into the kitchen. She scooped her keys off the counter and turned off the DVD player. The TV reverted back to a cable station as breaking news splashed across the screen. Senator Bonnie Clarkson was at the podium at the legendary Waldorf Astoria in New York City, giving a press conference in front of hundreds of her most starch supporters. The Senator captured Dougherty's attention, he couldn't put his finger on it at first, but there was something hauntingly familiar about her. And then it hit him like a bolt of lightning; he remembered all right, how could he forget? Dougherty had just seen her not eight hours ago at the farmhouse. He realized that Bonnie Clarkson was, in fact, Lilith, the powerful demon that escorted Jonas Payne back to the nether world. On the idiot tube, she looked more like a Republican front-runner than the queen of the succubus. Dougherty listened intensely as he caught the tail end of her speech.

"…I understand that this may be exceedingly premature, but I wanted to quill the swirling rumors and announce my candidacy for the President of the United States…," Clarkson offered as thunderous applauds and cheers rang out.

The television camera pulled back showing bedlam breaking out in the banquet room over the declaration. The camera pulled out further and a reporter came into view with his summation.

"So there you have it, Senator Bonnie Clarkson officially throwing her hat in the ring for the highest office in the land. Should be interesting as the field narrows. But with the election 16 months away, anything can happen…"

Myra turned off the television.

"Do you know that woman?" she asked skipping out of the apartment.

"No. I don't think so," Dougherty said not very convincingly as he followed the child.

Myra closed the door behind her and locked it.

"Is my father meeting us for breakfast?" she asked as they made their way down the hallway.

Dougherty withheld a reply and put his arm around the child. Through her loose fitting tank top, the beginnings of a new scenario imprinted across her fair skinned back.

EPILOGUE

The governing body of the Trenton Archdiocese called an emergency meeting. The elders present at the impromptu powwow were Bishop Terrence, Monsignor McElroy, Fathers Cobb, Clemens and Edwards as well as Deacon Izzo. The dignitaries sat in a semi circle and in the center of the action, on the hot seat, for the first time in his illustrious career was Monsignor Hayden. And also, for the first time in his career, Hayden feared that he might be in danger of losing his corner office.

"You wanted to see me, your Excellency?"

"With regards to Liam Dougherty, what exactly is his status in this Diocese?" Bishop Terrence asked, in a room that provided the perfect acoustics for his condescending tone. A room of marble upon marble that reeked of Vatican excess and was steeped in a rich tradition of Christian finger pointing. It was an inquisition all right, just as Hayden suspected.

"Regrettably, Mr. Dougherty has been relieved of his duties, sir." Hayden stuck to his guns, hoping there was a demand for a tired ex monsignor in charge of the supernatural department, on the lecture circuit.

"On what grounds, may I ask?" Terrence continued.

"He was found to be of questionable moral integrity. Sub standard behavior unbecoming of a priest."

"And what standard are you referring to?" Father Cobb inquired.

"Father?" Hayden asked confused.

"Let me rephrase that, is he still drinking?" Terrence asked directly.

"I would venture to say with reasonable certainty, that he is, yes."

Father Clemens fired a look at Deacon Izzo. His desire to go off the record was understood and Izzo stopped writing.

"We don't care about Dougherty's drinking," Clemens said.

"Are you aware that he rescued the kidnapped girl that was supposed to be under your care?" Bishop Terrence recapped.

"Well aware, yes, sir."

"And are you also aware that the media has declared him a hero?" Terrence added.

"No sir, I wasn't aware—"

"This Diocese has experienced a steep decline in fellowship." Bishop Terrence made his case. "Only 18.7 percent attend church regularly. Parish contributions are down by a third of what they were a year ago."

"It's understandable." Monsignor McElroy weighted in. "Lord knows we've had our share of bad press. People need hope. They need a reason to believe again. They need, quite frankly, for lack of a better word, a hero. A champion that will bring them to their knees again, worshiping in our pews."

"You simply can't buy this kind of positive spin." Terrence nodded. "Are we connecting, Monsignor Hayden?"

"I think so, sir," Hayden said, thinking about new additions to his corner office, like that 35-inch plasma television he had his eye on. And how crystal clear the Devil games will look in high definition.

"We're not suggesting that you bring him back unsupervised. By all means watch him," Father Edwards advised. "Watch him closely. But for God's sake, bring Liam Dougherty back. This Diocese can't afford not to."

"Will that be all, sir?" Hayden asked, thinking about not only the 35-inch television, but also perhaps a Wii for his niece as well?

"For now," Bishop Terrence said. "Thank you for your time, Monsignor Hayden. Peace be with you."

"And also with you, your Excellency."

With his marching orders in hand, Monsignor Hayden got up and walked out of the room, his heavy footsteps echoing every step of the way.

THE END